Private jets. Luxury cars. Exclusive five-star hotels. Designer outfits for every occasion and an entourage of staff to see to your every whim.

In this brand-new collection, ordinary women step into the world of the superrich and are

TAKEN BY THE MILLIONAIRE

Don't miss any of this month's offerings:

Mistress to the Tycoon
Nicola Marsh

At the Billionaire's Bidding
Trish Wylie

The Millionaire's Blackmail Bargain
Heidi Rice

Hired for the Boss's Bed
Robyn Grady

Dear Reader,

What is it that you love so much about Harlequin Presents Collections? Do particular themes have you on the edge of your seat? What does a sexy alpha male have to do to get your heart racing? You can share your views and find more information about books and authors at www.iheartpresents.com or you can e-mail us at presents@hmb.co.uk.

From next month, these collections will be known as Presents Extra. Be sure not to miss any of the titles in April 2008, when our heroines find themselves IN BED WITH THE BOSS!

Best wishes,

The Editors

MISTRESS TO THE TYCOON

NICOLA MARSH

TAKEN BY THE MILLIONAIRE

TORONTO • NEW YORK • LONDON
AMSTERDAM • PARIS • SYDNEY • HAMBURG
STOCKHOLM • ATHENS • TOKYO • MILAN • MADRID
PRAGUE • WARSAW • BUDAPEST • AUCKLAND

ISBN-13: 978-0-373-82071-9
ISBN-10: 0-373-82071-2

MISTRESS TO THE TYCOON

First North American Publication 2008.

Previously published in the U.K. under the title BIG-SHOT BACHELOR.

NICOLA MARSH has always had a passion for writing and reading. As a youngster, she devoured books when she should have been sleeping, and later kept a diary whose content could be an epic in itself!

These days, when she's not enjoying life with her husband and sons in her home city of Melbourne, she's at her computer, creating the romances she loves, in her dream job. Visit Nicola's Web site at www.nicolamarsh.com for the latest news of her books.

Nicola also writes for Harlequin Romance®.

For my editor Maddie,
who is fabulous to work with!

CHAPTER ONE

'COME in and take off all your clothes.'

Ariel Wallace grimaced at how forward that sounded and tried another tack.

'Make your way out the back. You'll find pegs to hang all your clothes on.'

Uh-uh. Worse.

'You've probably done this a thousand times before so head through that door, disrobe and let's get started.'

No hope!

Shaking her head, Ariel covered her face with her hands, not surprised to feel heat scorching her cheeks and deriving little comfort from the familiar smell of turpentine on her paint-splotched skin.

She couldn't do this.

Being an artist involved spontaneous bursts of creativity, fabulous blending of colours and frantic slashes of brushes, not inviting some guy she didn't know to get his gear off so she could paint him.

Whopping big commission or not.

She'd find some other way to keep Colour by Dreams afloat. She had to. She'd promised Aunt Barb, the founder of this amazing gallery and the woman who had practically raised her, that her legacy would live on.

And she'd do anything to make that happen.

The soft tinkle of wind chimes signalled a visitor entering the gallery and Ariel stiffened, her hands dropping from her face as she braced for an awkward confrontation. She knew how much uni students needed money and giving some poor guy the brush-off, no pun intended, didn't sit well with her.

If anyone knew about being poor, she did.

Which was exactly why she had to paint her first life portrait since art school. She had no choice.

'Hello? Anyone here?'

'Be there in a sec,' she called out, casting a final longing look at the back door, wishing she could make a quick dash for it.

Instead, she smoothed her favourite ochre peasant skirt, retied the Paisley bandanna under her unruly curls and pasted an I'm-in-charge-and-not-in-the-mood-for-nonsense look before stepping through the beaded curtain that separated her work area from the gallery out front.

'Miss Wallace? I'm Cooper—'

'Hi, Cooper. My studio's out the back so if you head out there, I'll lock up in here and be with you shortly.'

The words tumbled out in a rush, a combination of nerves, embarrassment and shock. She'd expected a lean, young, scruffy guy to come slinking into the gallery looking half as embarrassed as she felt.

Instead, she struggled not to stare at Cooper. She had no interest in his surname; she didn't want to get too personal considering she'd soon be seeing him in the buff.

Buff...
Naked...
In the raw...

She swallowed, unable to link those words with the guy standing in front of her. If she'd been mortified at painting some dishevelled, half-starved student without his clothes on, the thought of Cooper—all six-three, broad shoulders, long legs, killer smile, too-blue eyes and dark hair—sitting for her without a stitch on made her positively light-headed.

Though that could just be the oil-paint fumes.

'I wasn't sure you'd want to do this,' he said, amusement lighting his eyes, making them sparkle in the muted lights and sending an unexpected bolt of awareness through her.

'No choice.'

She stared, stunned by his easy confidence, his cool poise.

Wasn't this guy the teensiest bit embarrassed about getting naked before a stranger?

Judging by his confident smile and casual stance, obviously not.

'We always have a choice, Miss Wallace,' he said, his deep voice resounding in the high-ceilinged room, as sexy as the rest of him.

Darn it, and that was with his clothes on!

'Actually, I don't have a choice. If I can't capture you on canvas and sell the painting for the fortune I've been promised, I lose this place to some slime-ball developers who've been buying up the rest of this street.'

Confusion clouded his steady stare for a second before a tiny frown creased his brow and his smile vanished.

Great, she was scaring off prime model material before she'd even started.

Blowing a stray curl out of her eyes, she said, 'Look, I'm sorry to dump all that on you. I tend to babble when I'm nervous and, to be honest, I haven't done nudes in quite a while. Guess I'm a bit bashful.'

She averted her eyes and crossed the room, her beaded flip-flops slapping noisily against the polished Tasmanian oak boards, not wanting to see him staring at her as if she had two heads. Or, worse, laughing at her.

'You think I'm here to model?'

Flicking the door switch to locked and flipping the sign to 'closed', she swung back to face him, wishing she didn't need the money so desperately. Nothing was worth this awkward tenseness, even if he was the first guy to catch her attention in a long while.

'Well, aren't you?'

She flicked her gaze over him, starting at his almost-black hair worn a tad too long and curling at the collar of his navy polo shirt, over the snug way the shirt's cotton moulded his impressive chest and downwards, where faded denim encased long, lean legs.

No doubt about it. He was perfect model material, would be incredible to paint if those muscles hinted at beneath his clothes were as impressive as she thought. But there was something about him…something off-putting, as if he didn't belong here.

He paused, staring at her way too intently as if making up his mind about something.

Well, she would just have to make it up for him. She didn't have all night, and as much as she didn't want to do this, the sooner they made a start, the better.

'Look, I know this is probably awkward for both of us. Why don't I make us both a nice cup of honey and ginger tea? It'll help us relax and you can get changed behind that screen over there. I'll be back in a jiff.'

Ariel whirled around and headed into her studio, unable to fathom the stunned look in Cooper's blue eyes. She expected to hear his footsteps following her and when he didn't move, it suddenly hit her.

His confusion, his reticence: this had to be his first time doing this.

And she thought she was nervous!

Pausing in the doorway, she turned back to him, hoping to allay some of his discomfort.

'Cooper, if it makes you feel any better, you can keep your underwear on for this sitting,' she said, sending him her best smile, much cheerier now that she knew someone else in the room felt a lot more embarrassed about this whole fiasco than she did.

Cooper didn't move.

He couldn't.

He tried but both feet seemed firmly rooted to the spot as he watched the gypsy float through a curtain of shimmering purple glass beads after sending him the kind of bewitching smile that could make a guy seriously rethink his career.

After all, look at the way his mind was working at the moment. He'd gone from Melbourne's number one property developer to artist's model—nude model!—in less than a flash of pearly whites set against a luscious rosebud mouth.

He must be losing it.

All those extra hours at Vance Corporation trying to make a name for himself must've fried his brain.

This was obviously a silly case of mistaken identity and, the sooner he cleared it up, stated his business, secured what he'd come here for and headed back to the office, the sooner he could launch his own dreams.

'Cooper? Tea's ready. Come and get it.'

Squaring his shoulders, he pushed through the ridiculous dangling beads in the doorway, getting caught up in the process.

'Here you go.'

After disentangling himself, he finally looked up and stepped into Aladdin's cave.

At least, that was what it sure felt like to him: in each corner of the large room, swatches of gossamer-thin gold fabric hung from hooks on the ceiling and fell to the floor in cascading waves. Two ruby sofas sat at opposing ends of the room, covered in royal blue and purple cushions. There were unlit candles of all sizes, shapes and colours covering every available surface, both floor and glass-topped tables alike, while oil paintings of every description covered the walls.

The overall effect was bright, stunning and welcoming. Though that might have more to do with the gorgeous woman standing in the middle of the eclectic room with a strangely vulnerable smile flickering around her lush mouth.

'Drink some of this. It'll make you feel better.'

He took the chipped pottery cup, mentally searching for the right words. Maybe he should take a leaf out of her book and opt for brutal honesty? Something to the effect that he was the 'slime ball property developer buying out the street'?

Yeah, that would go down a treat.

Taking a tentative sip of the pungent brew—a brave move, considering he was a five espressos a day kind of guy and hated the herbal stuff—he tried not to stare at the woman standing between him and his own corporation.

'Good?'

'Mmm,' he said, surprised he didn't have to lie as the warm honey and spicy ginger slid across his tongue, giving his taste buds a pleasant jolt in the process.

'Drink up, then we can get started.'

He tried not to stare, he really did, but there was something about Ariel Wallace that drew his gaze like a connoisseur to a masterpiece.

She wasn't a beauty in the classic sense of the word, what with the crazy flowery bandanna covering her blonde curls, the heart-shaped face devoid of make-up, the pert nose and wary green eyes that looked as if she'd seen more than her fair share of trouble. As for her body, what little he could see of it beneath a voluminous ruffled skirt that matched her bandanna and loose white cotton top that hid more than it revealed, he couldn't pass judgement.

Okay, he couldn't see a lot of Ariel beyond her un-usually striking face and bizarre dress sense, but, somehow, the exotic combination and her unique style had captured his attention. Go figure. He found it par-ticularly strange when he usually admired elegantly dressed women, the bulk of his female acquaintances preferring black and expensive jewellery.

'Right. If you pop behind the screen and get ready, I'll get set up over there.'

Her brisk, no-nonsense tone had him hiding a smile behind his mug. She could be instructing him to take out the garbage rather than get naked.

Time to set the record straight.

'Miss Wallace, I don't think this is going to work. In fact, there's been a mistake—'

'No!'

She crossed the room in two seconds flat, standing toe to toe with him before he could blink. 'There's no mistake. I haven't got time to find another model. I need this painting done ASAP and that means you're staying, nerves or not. Got it?'

If she'd jabbed him in the chest, he wouldn't have been surprised.

'And call me Ariel.'

She stared at him, so close he could see the tiny gold flecks flickering in the green depths of her striking eyes, issuing a challenge he had no intention of taking up.

'I'm not nervous.'

Though with this crazy woman looking ready to deck him if he refused to get his gear off, maybe he should be.

'It's just that I'm not who you think I am.'

She quirked an eyebrow, a sassy elevation that drew his attention to her eyes again, their unusual crystal-clear green distracting him from the task at hand: set the record straight, seal this deal and get away from the office, his father and the memories.

'Look, Cooper, I don't care who you are. You could be the Crown Prince of Transylvania for all I care. Right now, I need you sitting on that stool, without any clothes on, staring out that window and holding the pose till I say move. Okay?'

'This is insane,' he muttered, admiring her sass and wondering if she'd deck him when he told her the truth.

She was close enough to do it. Way too close. Her intoxicating scent, the faintest hint of flowers and oranges, had to be playing havoc with his brain because for one, tiny, infinitesimal second, he almost considered doing what she said.

'No, you're insane if you think you're leaving here tonight before I get your form sketched. Now, shelve the shy act and let's get to it.'

She cast him one last challenging look before strutting to an easel about five feet away, busying herself with charcoals and paper to give him time to disrobe.

He must be mad.

Nuts, crazy, totally loco.

But then, considering how desperate he was to obtain this gallery, the last bit of prime real estate in Brunswick Street and his ticket out of Vance Corporation, maybe taking off his clothes for the crazy lady wouldn't be so bad.

'You ready yet?' she said without turning around.

'Almost.'

With a wry grin, Cooper headed for the ornate Japanese screen, pulling his T-shirt off along the way.

As a method to inveigle his way into a client's confidence, he'd never imagined getting naked.

Then again, this wasn't his fault. He'd tried to tell her the truth and she wouldn't listen. Ariel Wallace wanted a model and it looked as if he was it.

He just hoped she wouldn't spear him with the nearest paintbrush when she discovered he was here to pull the easel out from under her.

CHAPTER TWO

'DON'T move!'

Ariel picked up her third charcoal nub, tilted her head to get a better view of Cooper's impressive pecs and let her fingers fly across the paper, hoping to capture some of her model's essence before her aching hand gave out completely.

Easier said than done considering she'd never seen a guy's body like this before: all hard lines, delineated muscles and large expanses of smooth, tanned skin.

Wow.

'You've been sketching for an hour and I'm cramping. I've got to stretch my legs.'

'Oh, no, you don't.'

She fixed him with a glare, determined to get as much from this first sitting as possible. The less she saw of Cooper's toned body, the better. The thought of having to sit through more than a few evenings of seeing his muscles in all their glory made her break out in a cold sweat.

She really needed to get out more.

'You're a hard woman,' he muttered, shifting slightly

to the left as light fell across his right shoulder, creating intriguing shadows with his upper torso.

Magnificent.

If Sofia Montessori, Melbourne's society matriarch, wasn't happy with this commission, nothing would do.

'I'm a businesswoman. I guess being hard goes with the territory.'

She stared at his right clavicle, hoping she could capture the exact angle, not surprised she'd focussed all her attention on his upper body and virtually ignored his bottom half.

Even with boxer shorts—brief, black, poured-on boxer shorts—and his leg bent, heat flooded her cheeks at the thought of sketching Cooper in his entirety. Having such an impressive model had startled her enough for one night and she couldn't quite face drawing the whole 'life' bit in one setting.

'So you own this place?'

Happy to answer his question—anything to deflect her wandering attention away from those skimpy boxers—she said, 'Technically, yes. My aunt opened this gallery years ago and she left it to me when she died. But what with the recent fire in the storeroom, the sky-rocketing insurance premiums and the increasing over-heads, it's getting tougher to keep the place open.'

Not that she'd contemplate closing for one second. She owed Barb, her surrogate aunt, more than she could hope to repay.

'Sorry to hear about your aunt.'

Concern flickered across his face and he glanced away, not quite able to meet her eye as a ripple of unease slid down her spine.

Cooper looked almost…guilty? Couldn't be. What did some guy who didn't know her have to be guilty about? Must be her exhausted mind playing tricks on her. That, and the shock of his gorgeous bod sending her wow-factor off the scale.

'Thanks. Barb was amazing. Just ask anyone in the street.'

'How's that?'

'She fostered local talent and more. Barb rarely made a profit, donating huge chunks of money to charities and doing a lot with the street kids in the area.'

Such as taking in a runaway eight-year-old and giving her a home, something Ariel had never had before. 'She was a Brunswick Street icon.'

'Sounds like quite a lady.'

Touched by the admiration she heard in Cooper's voice, Ariel continued babbling about a subject close to her heart. 'That's why this particular portrait is so important to me. I need the cash to keep the gallery going and I need it yesterday. So if I seemed a bit pushy earlier on, I'm sorry.'

'Chalk it up to the temperamental artist, huh?'

'You got it.'

Ariel lifted her gaze from Cooper's shoulder to his face, hearing the gentle teasing in his voice and liking it way too much.

She didn't date much; she didn't socialise a lot. Keeping the gallery open and viable took up all her time and she liked it that way. Work she could rely on, people rarely.

Then what was it about this guy that had her wishing for something more? Wishing for an easygoing companion at the end of a hard day to listen to her rambling, to send her an encouraging smile when she needed it, to tease her?

'We're done,' she said all-too-briskly, snapping shut her box of charcoals and running a weary hand over her eyes, more to block out the sight of Cooper's body than anything else.

Now that she'd stopped working, seeing him almost naked took on an intimate connotation. The last thing she wanted or needed was to associate the words 'naked' and 'intimate' with him.

After all, she had at least another four sittings till the painting was complete.

'Great.'

He slid off the stool and she quickly averted her gaze, not wanting to see any more than she had to.

'So is it finished?'

'What?'

She sank back onto her ergonomic seat, blowing on the annoying curl that consistently fell across her eyes no matter how much she moussed, gelled or waxed it, relieved he'd popped behind the screen in record time.

'The painting. I take it I'm all done here?'

His voice drifted over the screen and she closed her eyes to savour the rich timber.

Great. Apart from needing to get out more, maybe she should air the studio a bit better. The paint and turpentine fumes were definitely affecting her.

'You really haven't done this before, have you?'

'Uh…no.'

He emerged from behind the screen and his presence struck her anew, his appeal not diminished in the slightest by clothes. Especially now she knew exactly what lay beneath.

'Well, let me clue you in. You sit, I sketch, draw, paint, whatever it takes to get this baby done. Tonight, I sketched your basic form but there's a lot more to be done.'

Like sketch his *whole* form. But she wouldn't think about that right now.

'I don't think—'

'You're not paid to think, you're paid to sit. So, how does tomorrow evening suit you?'

By the pained expression on his handsome face, it looked as if he equated having a wisdom tooth pulled without anaesthetic to posing for her again and she rushed on, not giving him an opportunity to refuse.

'No problems? Good. See you here at seven. You know the way out.'

Ariel bolted up the stairs to her apartment, waiting for the front door to shut before sidling down again.

After the inane chatter and light banter she'd exchanged with Cooper, the gallery's silence seemed almost oppressive.

Sighing, she flicked off the light switches, secured the front door and headed for the stairs.

However, the lure of seeing what she'd achieved pulled her towards her easel. Usually, she preferred to leave her work overnight and appraise it with a fresh eye in the morning, but not this time.

Maybe it was the unusual subject she'd worked with, maybe it was professional curiosity, but, whatever drew her to the myriad sketches she'd done of Cooper, the minute she laid eyes on what she'd drawn she wished she hadn't looked.

Though usually modest about her work, she'd captured the curve of his jaw, his high cheekbones, the breadth of his chest and his strong arms perfectly.

She inhaled sharply, half expecting the sketch to come to life and step off the paper and into her empty life.

It wasn't so much the thought of a guy like Cooper entering her life that scared her as much as the thought she might like it.

'How did things go with the Wallace woman? Get anywhere?'

Cooper nodded and handed his father a strong black, sugarless coffee just the way Eric Vance liked it.

'We met. I'm making inroads.'

Cooper hid a cynical grin behind his coffee mug, still not quite believing what had happened last night.

'What's that supposed to mean? Is she ready to sell? Because that's all I'm interested in, the bottom line here. That woman's been the bane of my existence for the last twelve months and if you're not up to the job, I'll find someone who is.'

His father glowered for extra effect, drank the scalding coffee in one go, yanked his leather chair out from behind his desk and plopped into it, his scowl deepening by the second.

'Rather than scare her off by barging in there, I'm taking a softer approach.' Unlike you, Cooper thought, but wisely kept that gem to himself.

Thankfully, he was nothing like his dad in the business arena, which was precisely why he had to get out of the company, the sooner the better.

'Waste of time,' Eric snapped, grabbing the nearest

object, which happened to be a gold pen, and tapping it relentlessly against the edge of his blackwood desk. 'Damn woman is stringing us along, hoping to get more cash out of us.'

Cooper stiffened. Though he hardly knew Ariel, she was nothing like the mercenary vulture his dad had made her out to be. From the top of her mussed curls to the bottom of her pale blue painted toenails, she'd appeared genuine, an artiste doing it tough but with a pretty clear goal: keep her gallery open in memory of its original owner, a family member.

Honourable enough, but then where did that leave him?

He couldn't weaken over this, no matter how much he'd admired Ariel and her convictions.

He had dreams of his own to build, starting with obtaining the very property she was trying to save.

'I'm handling it,' Cooper said, avoiding his father's assessing stare by striding to the huge glass windows overlooking Flinders Street Station and the Art Centre Spire behind it.

He loved Melbourne, really loved the hip, cosmopolitan feel of the city, the multicultural restaurants, the architecture. He'd acquired and developed many buildings since completing his MBA and each completed deal had brought him immense satisfaction.

Then why the slight niggle that obtaining the last prime bit of real estate in trendy Brunswick Street, Fitzroy, wouldn't be the be-all and end-all he'd first thought?

His father's sinister chuckle didn't reassure him. 'You're handling it, huh? Well, take as long as you like. I'm not the one who proposed some stupid deal in the first place.'

Cooper slowly clenched and unclenched his fists, hating how his father baited him on a daily basis, hating how it had come to this.

'We've talked about this. It's way past time I branched out on my own.'

'Fool idea! We can be a team here, and when I retire this whole company is yours.'

With Eric being a fit fifty-five, retirement was a long way off. Besides, Cooper was through working with dear old Dad.

'It's time I left and we both know it.'

Eric's eyes narrowed to cold, hard slits, his mutinous expression reminiscent of every time Cooper had disagreed with him since he'd turned ten. 'You signed a two-year contract when you first started. You've been here less than a year. I could make things tough for you.'

Cooper controlled his voice, hating the urge to shout. They'd had this same conversation every day for the last week, ever since his dad had failed to buy the gallery for the umpteenth time and Cooper had seized on the idea as his way out.

'Cut the empty threats. I seal the Brunswick deal, I'm out of my contract and on my own. You agreed, remember?'

'Of course I remember. You seem to think I'm stupid. Now, I've had enough of your *brilliant* ideas. Sit down and bring me up to speed with the Docklands deal.'

Shaking his head, Cooper turned away from the window and took a seat opposite his dad, who glared at him with angry blue eyes and a perpetual frown.

They'd been so close once: him and Dad. Laurel and Hardy, bouncing jokes off each other, getting a kick out of the same stuff: football, old western films, sailing. The Vance guys on top of their game.

His dad used to laugh a lot then, thriving on the thrill of an acquisition, sharing his success with him, enjoying a quiet celebratory beer together after work. Fishing holidays, blokes' weekends-away.

Then Cooper had joined the firm and started to make his own success in the business arena and his dad had changed. For the worse.

'The Docklands deal is almost completed. Contracts are in the legal department as we speak. So once I've got Ariel Wallace's go ahead and I wrap up the Brunswick deal, that's it. I'm done.'

For a second, something close to anguish flashed in his father's eyes. Before Cooper could fathom it, Eric blinked and his latent anger quickly replaced any other expression Cooper might've imagined.

'You'll never make it on your own.'

Cooper stood abruptly, keeping a tight leash on any number of fiery retorts and headed for the door and the sanctity of his own office.

'We'll see, Dad. We'll see,' he said, more determined than ever to get the deal done with Ariel Wallace.

CHAPTER THREE

'*CIAO, bella.* How's my favourite artist today?'

Sofia Montessori breezed into Colour by Dreams, her plump figure swathed in head to toe crimson, making her look like a ripe tomato. Ariel loved colour and Sofia's vibrant wardrobe never failed to brighten her day.

'I'm fine. How's life in the fast lane?'

'I can't complain. You know how it is. Places to go, people to meet, men to impress.'

'Actually, I don't know,' Ariel said, bracing for the on-slaught of Sofia's suffocating hugs and smacking kisses on both cheeks, smiling when she saw the usual match-making gleam in Sofia's dark eyes. 'And I like it that way!'

Sofia threw her hands up in the air and looked towards the heavens. '*Santa Maria!* You are young, you are beautiful. You should be partying, meeting men your own age, dancing the night away—'

'I'd rather paint the night away.' Ariel quickly cut in, knowing that once Sofia got on a roll, she'd be here all day. 'Speaking of which, I started on your commission last night. Want to take a look?'

'*Sì.* I want to see this life portrait that my sister is so keen on hanging in her house. Can you imagine, a naked man in the dining room? Ha! Enough to put me off my ravioli. But it's Maria's fortieth birthday and it's all she's talked about since she visited the National Art Gallery and what my baby sister wants she shall get.'

Sofia rolled her eyes and puffed out her cheeks in disgust and Ariel chuckled at her theatrics, knowing full well the rich Italian woman had a reputation as a connoisseur of younger men. Sofia was excited about this portrait and would probably order one for herself once she got a good look at Ariel's subject.

'I've only done a few preliminary sketches but you'll get the general idea,' Ariel said, pushing through the bead curtain leading to her studio and holding it up for Sofia to pass through, slightly nervous about the woman's reaction.

She rarely showed anyone her work before the final canvas but this was different. Sofia was paying her a small fortune and she didn't want anything to go wrong. She desperately needed the money. Like yesterday.

'They're over here.'

Ariel needn't have pointed. She knew the exact moment Sofia laid eyes on the sketches of Cooper.

'*Mamma mia!* Who is that?'

'That is the gift you're giving Maria.'

Ariel's casual wave of her hand didn't fool Sofia for a second.

'*Bella,* I know what *that* is. I want to know *who* that is.'

Ariel laughed at the predatory gleam in Sofia's eyes, which were round as pasta bowls.

'The model's name is Cooper. That's all I know.'

Actually, that was a lie.

She knew a heck of a lot more than that. Such as the way his blue eyes hid some sort of secret, as if he were ashamed of modelling.

And the way his muscles rippled when he moved.

And the way his deep voice had made her feel: like a woman who didn't have responsibilities, like a woman who could forget everything for the glimpse of his smile.

Sheesh! She really needed to start wearing a face mask to block the studio fumes from frying her brain.

'*Bellissimo!* This Cooper is gorgeous, no?'

'No. Yes. Oh, you know what I mean,' Ariel said, turning away from her sketches before her cheeks flushed crimson like Sofia's.

She didn't like admitting Cooper was gorgeous even if it was a fact. To her, the guy was work. A means to an end.

She just hoped she remembered it tonight when she had to sketch his bottom half.

'Is there more?'

Sofia's plucked eyebrows wiggled suggestively and Ariel knew exactly how much 'more' the older woman wanted to see.

'No, I haven't got to that part yet.'

And despite her earlier intentions not to blush, heat surged into her cheeks.

Sofia's ear-splitting grin didn't help. 'Ah…but I'm sure you're looking forward to it. If that part is as impressive as the rest, we're all in for a treat, no?'

'No!'

Sofia cackled and slipped an arm around her shoulders, the heady combination of expensive floral perfume and hairspray tickling Ariel's nose.

'You are a sweet girl, *bambina*. Why won't you accept money from me rather than paint men's bits?'

'We've been through this,' Ariel said, slipping from Sofia's claustrophobic embrace and crossing to an open window. 'You're a wonderful, kind woman but I can't accept your charity. I need to do this on my own.'

Sofia clucked and shook her head, sending mushrooms of hair product into the air while her bouffant didn't move a millimetre. 'Barb wouldn't have wanted you running yourself into the ground to keep the gallery open. She loved you too much.'

'And that's exactly why I have to continue her work. I've got Chelsea Lynch's first show coming up next week and Chelsea's exactly the type of local talent Barb would've busted a gut for. Chelsea's had a tough life, brought up on the streets around here, making good, finally doing something with her life. I need to be there for her, for all of them.'

Just as Aunt Barb had been there for her.

What the kind-hearted woman had ever seen in a rebellious eight-year-old street urchin Ariel would never know. From the first minute Barb had found her sleeping out the back of the gallery, wrapped in a paint-splattered canvas, Ariel had known nothing but patience and understanding and love.

She'd been one of the lucky ones and now it was her turn to give something back.

'You are a saint,' Sofia said, kissing her fingertips and blowing the kiss towards her.

'At the price I'm charging you for this commission, you think?'

Ariel's gaze drifted towards the sketches of Cooper,

wondering if her luck had finally changed when he'd walked in the door last night.

For her, art was about beauty, and though life portraits came in many shapes and forms, she knew that working with a perfect subject like Cooper would do a lot more for her inspiration than painting some recalcitrant, skinny guy.

And who knew? With a portrait of a great looking subject like Cooper hanging in the house of one of Melbourne's richest women, she might get inundated with commissions, meaning she could teach more classes, support more shows and do more for the local charities.

She'd make sure this was her best work, bits or not, if it killed her.

'Your work is beautiful, *bambina*. You don't charge nearly enough. Uh-uh!' Sofia held up a hand when Ariel opened her mouth to refute this. 'I will not hear another word. You do this painting for me, we talk some more then. Now, I must go. Antonio is taking me to a divine new trattoria in Lygon Street.'

'And who's Antonio?'

'A very sweet boy.' Sofia batted her long, mascara'd eyelashes and Ariel laughed, knowing Antonio would be young, handsome and pliable. '*Ciao, bella.* You have fun with your model, no?'

'No,' Ariel muttered, returning Sofia's continental kiss-on-each-cheek and hoping she could complete this portrait in record time.

Having fun with the model was the furthest thing from her mind.

At least, it should be.

* * *

Cooper stood outside the gallery, admiring the wide windows, cream rendered walls and green fretwork. He'd been past this site a thousand times over the last few months—even when his dad had been handling the acquisition through the local council. Each time, he'd been more intent on assessing the gallery's street position and how the space could be developed than aesthetics.

Colour by Dreams.

A nice name.

A name of hope and imagination and creativity.

Shame he had to tear it all down.

He'd never had qualms about business before, no point starting now, even if the gallery's owner had piqued his interest.

Pushing through the front door, he dodged the ridiculous wind chimes signalling his entry and hoped Ariel was in a receptive mood.

He had to tell her the truth before this farce went any further. Lying didn't sit well with him and he'd always been scrupulously honest in past deals.

Though where had that got him? Bound to his dad with the same ironclad contract all Vance employees signed, trying to be the best he could and now determined to get out.

'Hi, you're right on time.'

Ariel strolled into the gallery from the back, having little trouble with the silly beads dividing the rooms and he faltered, staggered by the power of her smile and the glint in her sparkling eyes.

Tonight, she wore a white ruffled shirt, a plum crushed velvet vest, black pleated shorts and pink wedges that made her legs look impossibly long. A crazy ensemble, which would've looked ridiculous on any other woman but on Ariel it looked like haute couture. She wore her clothes with aplomb and he smiled, thinking an eye patch wouldn't have looked out of place with her rakish pirate get-up.

'Something funny?'

'No, just admiring your outfit.'

To his amazement, she blushed, the hint of pink accentuating the green of her eyes and the rich gold of her hair, which she wore in a high pony-tail.

With her straightforward manner and sassy mouth, he hadn't thought she'd be prone to blushing.

'You like my taste in clothes? I find that hard to believe. Anyway, enough of the chit-chat. Let's get started.'

Hell. This was going to be harder than he'd thought.

He cleared his throat. 'Actually, that's what I want to talk to you about.'

'Oh, brother!' She rolled her eyes, plopped onto a stool behind the counter and rested her chin in her hands. 'Don't you think we moved past the whole virginal act last night?'

Cooper stared at her, torn between wanting to laugh out loud and call her bluff. Every time he tried to tell her the truth, she either interrupted him or came at him with some smart-ass remark.

He'd give it one more shot.

If she wouldn't listen, he'd shelve his good intentions and use tonight as one last opportunity to get some inside information on the opposition before approaching her with his plans for the gallery.

And when the time came, he wouldn't take no for an

answer, however cute the word sounded coming out of her sweet mouth.

'I think you should know more about me, listen to what I have to say—'

'Nope. Sorry. No can do.'

She jumped up from her stool, her ponytail bouncing like a jaunty flag amidships. 'Please don't take this the wrong way but I'm not interested in getting to know you. I'm not interested in you, period. You're here in a work capacity and that's it. You sit, I paint. End of story.'

She flounced past him, the same weird, intoxicating scent of flowers and oranges wafting over him, as enticing as the rest of her, and locked the front door.

End of story, huh?

Fine.

If Miss Bossy-Boots wouldn't give him a chance to explain, he'd take what he could from tonight and try the professional approach in the morning.

'On the contrary, the story is just beginning,' he murmured, following her into the studio with an extra spring to his step.

The man was a menace.

The harder she tried to concentrate on drawing the more he'd smile. Or fidget. Or want to chat.

She could strangle him with her bare hands.

Though she didn't want to get that close considering he wasn't wearing any clothes—bar the requisite boxers, which she'd insisted on again.

Chicken...

'So tell me more about this painting. Where's it going to hang?'

She silently cursed as her charcoal slewed off the paper. He'd spoken just as she'd captured the curve of his hip—and butt, but she didn't want to dwell on that piece of anatomy just yet. Time enough to study it, next sitting. Or the one after that...

'This is a private commission, a gift for a friend's sister, so it will hang in her home.'

'This isn't the fabled friend-of-a-friend thing, is it, and it's actually for your private collection?'

Ariel gritted her teeth, wondering if the use of duct tape over a model's mouth would be frowned upon by any worker's union.

'Sorry to disappoint, but this sort of art doesn't do it for me.'

'Then what does?'

Darn it, she'd been the queen of quick comebacks all her life. She'd had to be, living on the streets. But this guy fired back with a skill to be envied.

'None of your business, Mr Shy-and-retiring-before-whipping-off-your-clothes-in-record-time.'

'Hey, that's not fair. You practically shoved me behind that screen. I was terrified you'd actually rip them off me if I didn't get a move on.'

His smile did crazy things to her insides where her tummy flip-flopped and somersaulted and reminded her she hadn't eaten dinner. She'd tried before Cooper arrived but the thought of seeing all that gorgeous expanse of bare, tanned skin again had taken care of her appetite well and truly.

'You wish,' she said, aiming for a frown but failing miserably when their gazes locked over her easel and something zinged between them, an unspoken link, a zap of invisible electricity that made her heart join her tummy in the gymnastic stakes.

'Don't you ever shut up?'

Ariel's question sounded short and sharp in the loaded silence and she ducked behind the easel, buying valuable time to gather her wits and get her breathing under control. Alongside her pounding heart, her lungs had joined in the party and deprived her of much-needed oxygen.

Must be more of those nasty fumes affecting her again…

'It's pretty boring sitting here. A little conversation breaks the monotony.'

He sounded reasonable enough and she sneaked a peek, wondering if he was being serious or teasing her again.

To her mortification, he caught her furtive glance and winked, exacerbating her embarrassment no end.

She'd strangle him.

Once she'd captured his exquisite body—on canvas, that was.

'Have you always been an artist?'

She picked up a charcoal nub, determined to ignore him, but his question seemed innocuous enough and his voice had lost its teasing lilt.

'I loved drawing as a kid. I graduated from a black-board to chalk drawings on sidewalks. When other kids were playing hopscotch, I'd be sketching their faces. Later, I did a bachelor of arts to help on the teaching side of things but, basically, I worked alongside Barb here. We loved doing it…'

Her fingers stilled as she wondered what had possessed her to reveal so much to a guy she didn't know, a guy she didn't even particularly like all that much.

The cosy ambience of the studio at night seemed conducive to shared confidences but Cooper wasn't a friend and she'd be smarter remembering it.

'Anyway, that's it for now. I think I've done all I'm going to do tonight. Long day.'

She didn't look at him as she wiped her hands on a dusty rag, wishing he'd hurry up and get dressed so she could shove him out the door.

For a guy she hardly knew—and didn't want to know—Cooper had her in a spin, answering questions she'd usually ignore, deriving some comfort from confiding in another human being when she had so little social contact with anyone.

What a sad case.

'Ariel?'

'Yeah?'

She looked up, grateful he'd slipped into jeans and a white T-shirt quickly, obviously sensing her need to get rid of him without delay.

'Whatever happens, you should be proud of what you've done with this place.'

'Thanks,' she said, surprised by his serious expression and somewhat confused by what he'd said.

But she was too tired to think about it, let alone ask him to explain and she hurried him to the door, flicking the lock and all but wrenching it off its hinges in her haste to see the back of him.

As the door swung open and a chilly gust of wind blew it out of her hands several things happened at once.

Chelsea Lynch, her protégée, rushed into the gallery in a flurry of turquoise denim, red pashmina, emerald scarf and floppy fuchsia beanie.

Cooper took a polite step back, nodded at Chelsea and turned to Ariel. 'I'll see you tomorrow. We really need to talk.'

Ariel flashed him a tight smile, thinking her talking days with the too good-looking model were over if she had to finish his portrait with her sanity intact.

Chelsea's head swung between the two of them, her eyes wide with shock, her mouth hanging open before pointing an accusing finger at Cooper and shouting, 'What's he doing here?'

'Cooper's a model.'

'Like hell he is.'

Chelsea unwound her scarf in furious swirls, not taking her flashing hazel eyes off Cooper for a second. 'He's the scumbag who's been buying up the street and I bet he has his sights set on this place next.'

Ariel's protest died on her lips as she saw Cooper's stricken, guilty expression one second before her hand reached out, landed squarely in the middle of his broad chest and shoved him out the door.

Hard.

CHAPTER FOUR

ARIEL tried to slam the door in Cooper's face but took a second too long. The lying cretin stuck one of his shoes in the doorway and, as tempted as she was to amputate it, she couldn't afford a lawsuit on top of everything else at the minute.

'Get out!'

Ariel jiggled the door, hoping he'd get the hint, what with the way she'd shoved him out the door and now threatened to wedge his foot with it.

'Let me explain—'

'Explain what?'

She planted her hands on her hips, fury surging through her body at being taken for a fool.

When she'd been living on the streets as a youngster, people had always thought she was stupid, equating a dowdy appearance with nil intelligence, and she'd hated it.

She'd shown everyone and then some.

Exactly how she was going to show Cooper whatever-his-name-was—after giving him a verbal flaying he'd never forget, that was.

'I tried to tell you the truth a few times but you always shot me down, talked over me or didn't want to know,' said Cooper.

Ariel rolled her eyes. 'Give me a break! Guys like you can talk with a mouth full of marbles for business and you reckon you couldn't get the message across because I wouldn't let you? What a load of rubbish. You kept your big trap shut because you wanted to sleaze your way into my good graces. Isn't that right?'

'That's telling him,' Chelsea murmured, and Ariel sent her a quelling look to keep out of it.

Though she was grateful to her star pupil for outing the rat, she could fight her own battles. Always had, always would.

'Can we talk in private?' Cooper's steady gaze locked on hers, urgent, compelling, willing her to listen.

Too bad for him, she'd listened to enough of his lies already.

She shook her head. 'I'm not interested in anything you have to say. Now, if you don't mind removing your big foot from my door and shoving it back into your mouth, I have work to do.'

'This isn't the end,' Cooper said, sending her a look that meant business as he stepped out of the doorway.

'That's what you think.'

Ariel slammed the door, grateful for the double re-inforced glass: it saved her from shattering the windows and afforded a fantastic view of the priceless look on Cooper's face.

If she didn't know any better, she'd say he looked ashamed.

But that couldn't be right. Guys like him didn't have

a conscience and they never took no for an answer. They wheeled and dealed their way to the top regardless of the little people trampled in the process.

Well, she had news for him. This little person wouldn't let him near the place again, let alone buy it and ruin her plans for the future.

Cooper the marauding model could develop some other property, preferably in Timbuktu.

'Wow, that was awesome,' Chelsea said, slapping her on the back. 'You sure showed him who was boss.'

Suddenly fatigued, Ariel watched Cooper march up the street past the organic fruiterers, the vegan take-out and the Nepalese home-wares and turn the corner where he'd probably hidden some fancy sports car.

Lying louse.

Lying louse who had gotten under her skin in two short meetings.

And to make matters worse she had to work from memory to finish the portrait. The last thing she felt like doing was resurrecting memories of the louse's body and how great it would look on canvas.

'You okay?' Chelsea passed a hand in front of her eyes and Ariel focussed on the young girl.

'Yeah. How did you know who he was?'

'I've seen him around the Fitzroy area over the last few months. Mr Fancy-Schmancy works for a company that is responsible for ousting the Ngs from the corner grocer's, the Bortellis from their café and closing down the old Irish pub. All in the name of "development".' Chelsea held up her index fingers on both hands and made inverted comma signs. 'I hate guys like him. They've never done it tough. They don't know the first thing about the area or locals like me who live in it. They bulldoze their way in and rip lives apart. Tell me you won't let them get the gallery.'

Chelsea threw her arms wide and did a three-sixty. 'I love this place. All the local kids do. Barb made it more welcoming than any halfway house and you've continued the tradition. You can't let those bloodsuckers take it.'

Ariel managed a weary smile, buoyed by Chelsea's enthusiasm but more afraid than she'd ever been. She'd known about the property developers buying up every last piece of prime Brunswick Street land, but to hear Chelsea verbalise it somehow made the threat all the more real.

'Don't worry. I have no intention of letting them anywhere near Colour by Dreams.'

Chelsea clapped her hands like an excited child. 'Good, because my first showing is here in a week and I want the world to see my brilliance.'

'And your modesty,' Ariel said, trying to banish from her mind the threatening image of Cooper's final glower before he'd marched away and what it could mean for the gallery. 'Now, how about some tea and you tell me why you dropped by?'

Chelsea led the way out the back, bouncing with vitality, her pashmina trailing in her wake like a bright flag while Ariel followed, knowing it would take more than herbal tea to dispel her anxiety at the moment.

'Oh, wow!'

The minute Chelsea laid eyes on the preliminary portrait sketches Ariel had done of Cooper, she stopped dead in front of the easel.

'I'll take that as a compliment to my artistic skills and

not the subject in question,' Ariel said, busying herself making tea and hoping to God she had enough sketches for a final portrait.

Chelsea grinned, tearing her gaze from the sketches for a second. 'Don't get me wrong, I think you're the best artist this side of the Louvre, but wow-ee! That guy might be a slime-ball but he is one hot slime-ball.'

'I should've known he was too good to be true,' Ariel muttered, trying not to scald herself as she poured the boiling water into mugs, her hands shaking in anger at how Cooper had taken her in. 'Model, my butt.'

'Doesn't look like you got to that bit, worse luck.'

Chelsea winked as Ariel handed her a mug of steaming raspberry, the young woman's favourite. Ariel tentatively sipped at her peppermint brew, the steam heating her cheeks.

'Shouldn't be a problem. I can improvise.'

Sadly, Ariel knew her imagination wasn't *that* good.

'Whatever.'

Chelsea shrugged and took a seat on one of the ruby sofas, curling her long, legging-clad legs beneath her while she cradled her mug.

'Okay, Chelsea, what's up with you?'

Ariel didn't need any more problems right now. She had enough of her own to keep her busy into the next century.

'Do you really think I'm any good at all this art stuff?'

Chelsea's large hazel eyes radiated doubt and Ariel smiled, confident she could solve this easily.

Taking a seat next to the nineteen-year-old, she said, 'Do you trust my judgement?'

'Yeah.'

'And you know how tough it is to get a showing in Melbourne?'

The corners of Chelsea's mouth turned upwards. 'Yeah.'

'Plus you know how busy I am, right?'

Chelsea sat up straighter. 'Right.'

'Okay, you're a smart girl. Do you think I'd waste my time if I didn't think you're talented and inspired and are going to be the next big thing?'

'When you put it that way…' Chelsea plucked Ariel's mug out of her hand, deposited it next to her own on the floor and flung her arms around her. 'You're the best! Barb was so lucky to have someone like you take over for her.'

'I'm the lucky one,' Ariel murmured, blinking back sudden tears.

If only she could keep the likes of Cooper from taking away the only place she'd ever known as home, she'd be very lucky indeed.

'So where are we at with acquiring that gallery?'

Cooper refrained from glaring at his father, especially with a conference table full of developers, wishing his dad didn't keep pushing so hard. He'd said he'd handle it.

Yeah, like you handled it last night?

Silently cursing, he shuffled the papers in front of him and faced the curious looks of the men who'd invested millions into the project so far.

He'd give them what they wanted to hear before settling the deal one way or another.

'As you all know, Ariel Wallace isn't keen on selling. However, I've met with her the last two days and I'm optimistic she'll change her mind.'

She'd better. He needed to get out from this company and his dad's overbearing presence.

'What makes you think you'll succeed where I didn't?'

This time, Cooper couldn't stop his swift glare of condemnation at his dad. Sure, he knew Eric had taken professional jealousy to extremes, but did he have to air his feelings in this forum?

Quelling his anger, Cooper addressed the table at large. 'Eric, everyone here knows you're a top negotiator but I've established a rapport with Miss Wallace.'

Yeah, they'd grown real close if her shoving him out the door constituted camaraderie. 'I'm confident that, with a few more meetings, she'll come to the party.'

His farewell party, that was.

The day she signed on the dotted line was the day he would be free: free of his contract, free of Vance Corp, free of seeing the edge in his dad's eyes every time he walked into the room.

'Good.' Eric barely inclined his head in Cooper's direction before continuing. 'I've sealed the deal on several properties around the block from the gallery and we need that piece of land.'

Eric stabbed at a remote and a screen lit up with a PowerPoint presentation behind him. 'These are the preliminary plans, but once we secure the gallery we can demolish it along with the old houses behind it and create a six-storey apartment block. With property prices at an all-time high in suburbs surrounding the Central Business District, that's a killing for us.'

Eric stared at Cooper with contempt, as if saying, *And you want to leave all this behind? You think you can match me? Beat me at my own game?*

'Any questions?'

Cooper met his father's gaze directly.

He settled for keeping the peace just as he had every day for the last ten months since he'd graduated and signed on the dotted line with his father's company. He'd been full of ideals, full of enthusiasm and his father's attitude had whittled it away to this: a ridiculous trade so he could back out of his legally binding contract.

'The plans look good. I'm just as eager to get this deal done as all of you so perhaps we can reconvene next week?'

That should give him enough time to talk sense into the bohemian harridan who'd tossed him out like yesterday's garbage. He'd make sure of it.

'Fine. Meeting adjourned.' Eric headed straight for the built-in bar in the corner of the conference room where Cooper knew he'd swap shop talk with his cronies over a bourbon or two.

Not for him.

He had more important things to do with his time, such as getting Ariel to listen to his pitch.

If he were a betting man, he'd place a hundred on the nose that she wouldn't open her door to him again, let alone hear what he had to say.

Well, he planned to change all that.

Starting now.

CHAPTER FIVE

'YOU despicable low-life!'

Ariel slashed at the canvas with her brush, streaking across the blank expanse while glaring at the sketch of Cooper propped next to it.

She'd been trying to capture his likeness on canvas all morning and had tense shoulders, a tight neck and three ruined canvases—all recycled, thank goodness—for her trouble.

Her muse had deserted her.

Unfortunately, she had a sneaking suspicion her muse had hitched a ride on the despicable low-life's broad shoulders and cruised straight out the door.

She'd tried everything: burning her lime and tangerine candles for concentration, dabbing neroli—her favourite scent—on her pulse points for inspiration and to calm her mind, wearing her lucky holly garland on her head and a five-minute meditation which usually worked wonders if her imagination clogged.

The result?

Nothing.

And to make matters worse, Sofia had rung, gushing

about some fancy charity do at her sister's place where everyone who was anyone would see the portrait and inundate her with work—she wished—and imploring her to finish it a week early.

Which gave her exactly six days to get the portrait finished.

Would've been a cinch if she'd had a normal model and not some delusional businessman happy to whip off his clothes to get what he wanted, the lunatic.

Staring at the sketches of Cooper, she could've happily drawn devil's horns and pointy fangs all over his smug face, but they were all she had…and that wasn't much.

Sighing, she closed her eyes, trying to conjure up the memory of his form, hoping to translate it to canvas. Deep blue eyes, too long dark hair, strong jaw, broad chest, great pecs, tapered waist, long legs…magnificent…

The wind chimes over the front door tinkled and her eyes flew open. To her annoyance, a stupid little smile had snuck up on her and she wiped it, along with her too real—and too hot—images of Cooper's amazing body out of her mind.

'Can I help you…?' The rest of her words trailed into insignificance as the object of her vivid imagination a second earlier strutted into the gallery, the epitome of the slick businessman she now knew him to be: fancy suit, white shirt, duck-egg blue tie that matched his striking eyes. He looked amazing, but she preferred him in jeans and T-shirt.

Are you insane?

That was right, she didn't prefer him at all. Or was that in nothing at all?

'Go away,' she said, planting both hands on the counter and glaring at him with as much disdain as she could muster.

'No can do.'

He stopped exactly opposite and Ariel suddenly wished the too-thin glass-topped counter were wider.

He was too close, too masculine, too everything.

'I have a proposal for you.'

'After two nights? Gee, you must be really desperate to get this place but, sorry, I wouldn't marry you if you gargled a litre of turpentine and painted the street red.'

He gave her an arrogant smile that screamed 'bring it on'.

'You know I'm not here with a marriage proposal. You strike me as a smart woman and in the interests of your business I thought you should hear me out.'

'You thought wrong,' she blurted, not ready to hear anything he had to say.

She was too angry with him: angry he'd lied, angry he'd ruined a project so vital to the viability of the gallery, but most of all, angry with herself for the slight, inane leap of joy she'd experienced when she'd walked through the beaded curtain and seen he'd come back.

He ignored her petulant outburst. 'This will only take five minutes of your time. Believe me, it's important.'

She wouldn't believe him if he were the last man on earth. Still, something about his steady gaze and intense expression had her shrugging her shoulders and leading him out the back.

'Five minutes,' she said, propping herself on her ergonomic stool, not caring if he stood or sat. He wouldn't be around that long if she had anything to do with it.

'What's that on your head?'

Hmm…not exactly what Cooper had in mind as a stunning opening to his pitch, but he couldn't talk sense to a woman wearing a Christmas wreath on her head, even if she wore it with the aplomb of a queen sporting a priceless tiara.

Ariel frowned and patted her head, the frown disappearing when she touched the weird crown.

'This is my lucky garland. I often paint in it.'

'It looks like a Christmas tree gone wrong.'

Rather than taking it off her head in embarrassment as he expected, she adjusted the angle till it sat like a crazy halo perched at odds with her curls.

'I made it years ago during my first Christmas with Aunt Barb.'

Cooper wished he hadn't seen the vulnerability behind her eyes.

He was here on business. To present a clear plan to benefit them both. He didn't want to hear about this woman Barb whom Ariel held in such high esteem or feel the slightest twinge of guilt that in following his own dreams he'd probably have to tear hers down.

She was young. She'd get over it. Take the money, start a new gallery somewhere else.

'Your five minutes started about thirty seconds ago so whatever you have to say, make it snappy.' Ariel's expression had hardened, her green eyes flinty, her mouth compressed in a thin line.

Squaring his shoulders, confident a softer approach would work rather than railroading her as he usually did the rest of his clients, Cooper met her cool gaze head on. 'Firstly, I'd like to apologise for not telling you the truth earlier. You were right, I had plenty of opportunity and could've let you in on my identity sooner.'

'Why didn't you?'

'Honestly? You intrigued me. I had my spiel all worked out when I first walked in here, but before I knew what was happening you'd bustled me out the back and told me to take off my clothes. Guess the Neanderthal male in me took over and I kind of liked it. The whole situation was extraordinary and once we started talking, I couldn't leave.'

He opted for honesty, hoping the truth would convince her he was on the up and up now. By her unchanging expression, it didn't look as if it had worked.

'More like you didn't want to leave because you thought you could weasel inside info out of me before homing in for the kill.'

'That too. Pretty despicable but I was going to tell you the truth even if that girl hadn't outed me.'

She rolled her eyes before tapping her watch. 'Three minutes left.'

'Okay, my idea is this. I have a business proposal to present to you. It will probably take a few hours all up to do it justice and I was hoping you'd give me the time.'

'No.'

Short and sharp, without the slightest hint of thawing towards him in sight, and he pushed on, hoping she understood how things worked in the business world and wouldn't be offended by his next offer.

'I'll pay you for your time.'

'What?'

If her eyebrows shot any higher, they'd tangle in the wreath still perched on her wayward curls.

'In the world I come from, everyone charges by the hour, from lawyers to architects. I see your time as being no different and I'm willing to compensate you for the few hours it takes to deliver my pitch.'

'You're willing to compensate me…how *generous*.'

By her strange, high-pitched fake voice and the clenched hands twisting the cuffs of her crushed velvet shorts, he knew she didn't think his offer was that generous.

'The point I'm trying to make is that this place is your business, your time is just as valuable as everyone else's and I want to recognise that.'

Better, much better, and by the softening of her ramrod-straight posture, she thought so too.

'I don't want your money.'

'You'll still listen to my pitch?'

He held his breath, wishing this bohemian beauty didn't hold his future in the palm of her paint-stained hand.

She had to listen to his pitch and she had to go for it.

He couldn't contemplate any other outcome.

Starting out on his own after a lengthy legal battle to escape the contract would drive an irreversible wedge between him and his father.

Suddenly, Ariel's face cleared. Her brow smoothed, her lips tilted up at the corners and her green eyes sparkled with excitement.

Oh-oh. This couldn't be good.

He'd seen that same look when she'd all but pushed him into her studio the first night and told him to get his gear off.

'I won't accept your money but how about we do a fair trade for time?'

'Sounds feasible,' he said, not liking the smug expression spreading across her beautiful, unmade-up face.

He liked the tense, uncertain Ariel a lot more than her cheeky counterpart who made him want to drop his business ideals at the door and get creative with her in a variety of imaginative ways.

'What did you have in mind?'

To his surprise, Ariel slid off her stool and crossed the space between them, placing a finger under his chin and tilting his head this way and that.

'Yes, yes, yes!'

She dropped her hand and stepped back, continuing to study him like a prized masterpiece.

'This is perfect!'

She clapped her hands and smiled at him, the type of mega watt smile that could melt a guy's hardened heart if he wasn't careful. 'You pose for me till I finish the portrait and I'll listen to your boring proposal. How's that for fair trade? A few hours' modelling for a few hours of hearing you run off at the mouth?'

Cooper stared at her, unwillingly admiring her glowing eyes, her wide, confident smile. He bit back his first gut response of 'no way' knowing that a smart businessman would take every opportunity that came his way and turn it into something big.

In this case, it might be the only chance he got.

She'd let him in the door, she'd heard him out and she'd agreed to listen to his plans for this place.

Sitting in the near-buff, albeit on a damn hard stool, for a few hours would be nothing if he pulled this off.

'You've got a deal.'

He held out his hand, managing a genuine smile

when she placed her tiny hand in his despite the jolt physical contact brought.

By the slight widening of her eyes, she felt it too but pulled away before he could analyse it further.

Not that he wanted to. She wasn't his type.

He preferred cool, aloof women who were happy with the occasional date and had no expectations.

A warm, vibrant, creative woman like Ariel would be nothing but trouble for a level-headed guy like him and he'd make sure he concentrated on business around her.

He didn't have room in his life for anything else.

'Herbal tea is better for you,' Ariel said, trying to subdue her triumphant grin and failing as she bustled about the tiny kitchen off her studio.

Twisting Cooper's proposal to suit her own ends had come to her in a flash of brilliance and the way she saw it, she had it made. She'd get to finish the portrait and collect the much needed money for it and, in exchange, she'd spend a few boring hours listen to him prattle on about his plans for her gallery, plans that would never see the light of day if she had anything to do with it.

Easy.

'I'll stick with coffee, thanks.'

'Suit yourself,' she said, handing him the steaming mug of decaf he'd requested, knowing he'd find it lacking. He looked like a double espresso hold-the-milk-and-sugar type of guy to her. 'Speaking of which, you're looking a lot more uptight in that get-up than the other night. What were you trying to do then—con the crazy artist in your slumming clothes?'

His mouth twitched. 'I happen to live in jeans and T-shirts outside the office.'

'And?'

'And I thought you wouldn't be as intimidated if I turned up dressed casual.'

Ariel smiled. The guy was sneaky. And sexy, way too sexy.

'Wow, you better be careful, Mr Big-Shot. That's the second time in half an hour you've sounded honest. Didn't think your type had it in you.'

'If you're trying to bait me, forget it. I've got a thick skin. Comes with taking off my clothes for twisted women posing as artists.'

Okay, so the guy had a sense of humour. Lucky for him. He'd need it when she knocked his business proposal for the gallery on its head.

'The human body is a work of art. I can't help it if your head's filled with taking over buildings and ruining people's lives rather than appreciating the finer things in life in the way I do.'

She kept her tone light, enjoying trading banter with someone who could match her, even though her quip had a barb of truth to it.

She would never understand how he could barge into people's lives and turn them upside down with scant regard for the little people. Sure, he probably justified his actions with money but then that was all a success-ful guy like him understood.

'Have you ever considered I improve people's lives rather than ruin them?'

He took a sip of coffee and grimaced, hiding his distaste behind a discreet cough.

'Whatever lets you sleep at night.'

She drained her cup of peppermint tea and peered into the bottom, a silly old habit considering she'd switched to bags and didn't use loose leaves any more. Too bad—she could use a bit of forecasting right about now: such as how the portrait would turn out, would she keep the gallery, would she be able to keep her interest in the model purely professional?

'Would you like a refill before we get down to the nitty gritties and establish a few ground rules?'

'No, thanks.'

He beat a hasty path to the kitchen where he rinsed his mug in record time as Ariel followed at a slower pace, chuckling softly. He thought she'd assume he was being super helpful but she knew better; she'd seen his three-quarters-full mug and what better way to surreptitiously tip the whole lot down the sink than pretend to wash?

'What's this about ground rules?'

He dwarfed her kitchenette and she waited till he moved away from the sink before rinsing her own mug. She'd jokingly called him Mr Big-Shot but Cooper was just that, big in every way. It was more than a size thing, though; it was something about his supreme confidence, his imposing aura, the way he carried himself.

Usually, guys like him intimidated her, but Cooper had an innate kindness she sensed, an indefinable quality that drew her to him even if she kicked and screamed all the way.

Drying her hands on a tea towel, she resisted the urge to flick it at him as he turned away and walked out of the kitchenette. What was it about this guy that brought out her impish side?

The funny thing was, now they'd established where things were going and she'd got her way with the portrait, she couldn't stop teasing him and trying to get him to loosen up.

'Would you like to take a seat and we can discuss this?'

He shook his head and glanced at his watch. 'Can we make this snappy? I've already been here longer than anticipated.'

So much for teasing and lightening up.

'Fine. I just wanted to make sure we both understand the time involved in our trade. I probably need you to sit for another four sessions, about an hour each. How long will your pitch take?'

'Around two, but that's fine. When I make a deal, I stick to it.'

He folded his arms, the fingers on his right hand drumming ever so slightly against his left bicep. If he'd started tapping his feet, whistling and staring at the ceiling in impatience, she wouldn't have been surprised.

Talk about Jekyll and Hyde. The guy switched from light banter to cold indifference in a flash. The decaf must've really irked.

'Good. As for the posing part, you know it's a life portrait?'

She couldn't resist pushing his buttons.

'So you've told me.'

He didn't obviously look embarrassed, but a faint pink definitely stained his tanned cheeks.

'Just to put your mind at ease, you won't have to get completely naked. What you've been doing so far is great, with your leg covering, uh…'

Great, now it was her turn to blush. 'Anyway, I just

have to do the bottom half, then get some really
detailed sketches of your hands, feet and face and
transfer the whole lot onto canvas. Once I've finished,
I'll hear your pitch.' *And see the back of you, literally.*
'You okay with all that?'

'Fine. Can we get started tonight?'

He hadn't lost his antsy look. If anything, it had inten-
sified. Boy, he must really want her to hear his proposal.

'See you back here at seven.'

'Good. See you then.'

With a mock half-salute, he all but ran out of the
studio, through the gallery and towards the front door.

'Cooper, I forgot something.'

He paused with his hand on the doorknob. 'What's
that?'

'Bring a fig leaf. It might come in handy for camou-
flage.'

She tried to keep a straight face and couldn't, her
laughter following him out the door as his exasperated
expression told her exactly what he thought of her
sense of humour.

CHAPTER SIX

'CAN I take a look?'

Cooper wiggled his fingers and toes in an effort to restore circulation to his extremities, grateful that this modelling gig would be over soon.

Not that he didn't enjoy spending one-on-one time with Ariel, who surprised him at every turn, but he needed to seal the deal before next Friday. He had a feeling the investors wouldn't be too impressed if he stalled again.

As for his dad, he'd been close to up and leaving, contract or not, several times this week. They didn't just not see eye to eye any more, they seemed to be on a different plane altogether.

'Stop moving! I need to capture the arch of your right foot tonight and I'm done.'

She glared at him over the easel, dabbing her brush in the paints on a worn palette next to her before returning her attention to the canvas.

Even with a smudge of paint on her cheek, her curls escaping their customary bandanna—zebra stripes tonight—and falling across her forehead, and dark circles under her eyes courtesy of how hard she was pushing to finish this portrait in record time, she was the most beautiful woman he'd ever seen.

From the bottom of her pink raffia ballet shoes to her broderie-anglaise bolero worn over a chartreuse ribbed singlet, she looked adorable, a bright spark in his otherwise dull day.

As for those shorts she wore…for the last three nights, tonight included, he'd been subjected to long, gorgeous legs poking out from truly ugly shorts. Vintage tartan checks, awful blue flowers against mustard backgrounds and purple polka dots against turquoise. Thankfully, her eccentric taste in clothes hadn't blinded him to the beauty of her luscious legs and he'd done a fair bit of his own looking while she'd been studying him.

'When you say you're done, is that done as in finished completely?'

'You wish,' she said, absentmindedly twisting a curl around a finger while dabbing at the canvas.

Actually, he didn't.

The logical, business side of his brain was yelling 'woo-hoo' but the emotional side he'd deliberately shut down wished they could stay ensconced in her cosy studio for ever.

'How much longer?'

Exhaling loudly, she stabbed her brush into a glass jar of water, rolled her neck a few times, stood up and arched her back. 'Anyone ever tell you you talk too much?'

'Anyone ever tell you you're great at avoiding answering questions?'

After another catlike stretch, which had him averting his eyes in record time when she finally looked at him, she said, 'If you must know, I'm pretty much done. I just need to get a few details of your face completed and that's it.'

'Tonight?'

His heart sank. As much as he liked being here, he'd had a long day at the office and needed to finalise a report for a presentation first thing Monday morning.

She laughed, a genuine loud, throaty chuckle that made him want to join in. 'With you sounding so enthusiastic, I guess not. Why don't you get dressed and I'll make us a hot drink?'

Cooper tried not to screw up his face. If he had to endure one more cup of her foul-tasting herbal brews or equally horrid coffee, he'd happily walk away from this deal here and now.

'I've got a better idea. Why don't we grab a coffee at the café across the street? The place looks new; they could probably do with the business.'

'Before you tear it down, you mean?'

Her smile had vanished and he couldn't tell if she was serious or joking. Either way, he was too tired to argue.

'Whatever you decide to do, I'm heading over there for the largest strong black they've got. I have a long night ahead of me.'

A flicker of remorse crossed her face and she disguised it by tidying up her work space. 'Hot date, huh?'

'Yeah, the hottest,' he said, sliding his oldest cotton T-shirt over his head and slipping into faded denim. 'Just my slinky little laptop and me.'

'Do you enjoy what you do?'

He stepped out from behind the screen to find her perched on the stool he'd just vacated, a curious look on her paint-smudged face and her spectacular legs tucked up on the rung underneath.

'It's challenging. I like seeing things develop and take shape from the infant stages right through to the finished product. You can identify with that, surely?'

He expected a vehement rebuttal, but to his surprise she nodded, a tiny frown between her brows as if she was pondering what he'd said.

'Yeah, I can. Apart from the whole creative side of art, I love seeing something develop before my eyes. It's often hard work but the reward is worth it.'

'Exactly.'

They locked stares, his challenging, hers curious.

However, before she could chastise him any more for being a developer or tease him about his uptight ways, he turned away and shrugged into his leather jacket.

'Right, I have a mega-strong black with my name all over it. I'm out of here.'

He sent her a casual wave, a major part of him wishing she'd join him. Sure, they'd chatted a fair bit while she'd worked but he still didn't know what made her tick. She'd deliberately kept things light between them and he hadn't pushed, despite hoping to get more of an idea behind her absolute refusal to sell the gallery.

There had to be more to it, more than a promise to a dead aunt.

He'd bide his time, knowing the pitch he'd prepared to deliver would convince her. If there was one thing he had learned, the gorgeous woman with the kooky dress sense had a brain in her head, and hopefully, she'd see his proposal for what it was: good business, smart business and a win-win solution for them all.

He'd barely taken a step when she slid off the stool, picked up a giant straw holdall that looked like it could easily contain the proverbial sink and then some, and smoothed her wrinkled shorts.

'I think I'll come with you. I've been cooped up in this place working every night for a week straight. A change of scene will do me good.'

'So it's not my scintillating company that enticed you to join me?'

'Honestly? No.'

She matched his sardonic expression, tilting her chin up to meet his gaze head-on.

The minute he reached out to touch her cheek, he knew it was a mistake.

'You have a paint smudge right here.'

But then, he'd hardly been his usual rational, conventional self since setting foot in this place.

He slid his finger down her cheek, slowly, gently, her velvety smooth skin a magnet to his touch.

He should've pulled away the second her luminous green eyes widened and her lush mouth formed a small O, but instead he lingered, savouring the close contact, the intimacy enveloping them as surely as the heady perfume she wore.

'Th-thanks,' she said, stepping away to rub at her cheek, her eyes not leaving his. 'Just give me a second to get cleaned up and I'll be right with you.'

'No problems.'

However, he lied.

His reaction to the beautiful artist was definitely a problem, a major one.

He had no qualms about her focussing on the

business side of the deal he proposed, but the million dollar question was, could he?

Ariel snuggled into the comfy lounge-style chair, loving the homely ambience of The Cypress Tree. The new owners had done wonders with the place and she wasn't surprised to see it packed on a Friday night.

'What'll you have?'

'I'll have a decaf skinny soy latte, please.'

Cooper stared at her in disbelief. 'You're kidding, right? Tell me that's not a real drink.'

Ariel chuckled. 'To a boring, caffeine-swilling, strong black coffee hick like you, I guess not.'

Shaking his head, he placed their order with a waitress sporting a magenta Mohawk and enough facial piercings to keep the local silversmiths in business for the next decade. Though the punk hairstyle didn't do much for her, Ariel admired the teenager's gold lamé hot-pants and wanted to ask her which boutique she frequented.

'At the risk of sounding like the hick you just accused me of being, is it fancy-dress night at this place?'

Ariel smiled, knowing exactly what he meant but wanting to tease him a little. 'Why would you say that?'

Cooper's gaze traversed the cosy café, his eyes growing wider by the minute. 'For starters, there's a guy over there wearing cow-print leather pants and a red vest with nothing underneath. Then there's another guy wearing orange leather chaps over denim shorts. Throw in the overabundance of black spandex, gold sequins and silver metallic objects protruding from every body part imaginable, and do you blame me for asking?'

Ariel shrugged, suddenly saddened by the huge gulf between them. They really were from opposite ends of the planet in every way: their tastes, their occupations, their thinking.

Yet she still found him attractive. Go figure?

Darn hormones!

'I don't blame you for asking. I'm not surprised a man like you wouldn't know about a cultural hub like Brunswick Street. Take another look around.'

She swept her hand wide in an all-encompassing gesture. 'This place is where it's at. Hip, funky, brimming with life. If you took a walk up the street and actually looked into the buildings rather than dreaming about tearing them down, you'd see a hundred places like this. Jazz bars, tapas bars, Latin American clubs, comedy clubs and restaurants from all around the world. It's a hub of incredible contrasts and I love it.'

'You really think I'm some sort of ruthless cretin, don't you?'

He spoke softly and she had to lean forward to hear him over the din of chattering patrons and Spanish guitar music.

Thankfully, the waitress arrived at that moment and deposited two enormous steaming mugs in front of them, giving her time to phrase her answer carefully. She wanted to be honest but something about his watchful, brooding expression told her that now wasn't the time to be too brutal.

'Look, I have this habit of shooting off at the mouth. You know, honesty is the best policy and all that. Guess I just realised exactly how different we are.'

Ariel made a mad grab at her latte and took a huge

sip, scalding or not. There was *honesty* and there was honesty and from what she'd just said, he might take it she was interested in him. If she burned her tongue on the hot coffee, it mightn't be a bad thing. She might actually shut up for two seconds.

'You got that right,' he said, a speculative gleam in his eyes.

Great. The guy wasn't stupid and he'd picked up on her interest just as she'd suspected.

'One more session should see us done,' she said, gratefully hiding behind her latte mug.

'Make that two sessions.'

'Pardon?'

'One for you, one for me. My business proposal? Remember, that one tiny detail you seem to have forgotten?'

'Oh, *that*. You're right, minor details.' She smiled, showing she intended no malice. 'Maybe I'll be too exhausted after finishing the portrait to hear what you've got to say.'

'And maybe I'll spread nasty rumours about the artist getting up close and personal with her model.'

'You wouldn't dare!'

'Try me.'

By his challenging smile, she knew he was kidding but somehow, she didn't want to test him. Besides, the thought of what he'd suggested sounded way too good.

'Do you always get the final word?'

She could've backed down but then, where was the fun in that? If there was one thing guaranteed to get her fired up it was a challenge, particularly from a guy who probably always got what he wanted.

Rather than answering her mild dig, he changed the subject altogether.

'You mentioned earlier that all you need to finish is some facial details?'

'Uh-huh.'

'Do we have to do that in the studio?'

He finally reached for his coffee and drained the mug in one go, when what she really wanted to see was his entire face and read where a strange question like that was leading.

'The studio is where I do my portrait work.'

Though that wasn't entirely true. She'd often taken a sketch pad down to the St Kilda foreshore or Albert Park Lake, capturing whatever scene took her fancy whether it be a person, animal or view. New surroundings inspired her and she loved it.

But, somehow, the thought of sketching Cooper outside her studio seemed way too personal.

Like this.

One-on-one time in a cosy café, sitting across from his sexy smiles and piercing blue eyes, definitely entered the realm of too personal and made her forget one very important point.

This guy was the enemy.

No matter how charming, how glib, how sexy, he was here for one reason and one reason only: to tear her world apart. And she'd be a darn sight smarter to concentrate on that salient fact rather than the intense colour of his eyes.

'Too bad. Seeing as tomorrow is the weekend and it promises to be a perfect one, I thought it would be good to get a change of scenery. Don't know about you but I need to shake off my moon tan and catch some sun.'

He held his chin and turned his face from side to side, a half-smile on his face. 'It would be a good opportunity for you to study my exceptional profile in some real light. You know, to put the finishing touches on the masterpiece and all.'

She shouldn't encourage him, she really shouldn't.

But who could resist a man with a smart mouth like that?

'Where did you have in mind?'

Cooper winked and tapped the side of his nose in true conspirator fashion. 'Why don't you leave that up to me? Who knows, this boring hick might surprise you yet. Pick you up on Sunday around ten.'

With that he stood up, took a final glance around the café, sent her a sexy smile and headed out the door, leaving her wondering if she'd taken leave of her senses.

Painting Cooper was one thing.

Spending Sunday morning with the infuriating man, another.

Think of the finished portrait...think of the money...

Instead, all she could think about was how denim did incredible things to his butt and how stupid she was for noticing.

Worse yet, how in just under a week she liked this guy more than she'd liked any guy before.

Not good.

And she had a feeling that by spending her precious Sunday morning with him, things were about to get a whole lot worse.

CHAPTER SEVEN

'WELL, aren't you just full of original ideas this morning?'

Cooper smiled at Ariel and held open the door to Hideout, the funkiest café he could find in Brunswick Street. 'Hey, you were the one who said I needed to check out what this precinct has to offer, so here we are.'

'Wise guy,' she said, her smile warming him better than the sun's rays had for the last hour while he'd sat on Brighton Beach, more relaxed than he'd been in a long while as she'd studied his face, her fingers flying over her sketch-pad to capture his likeness.

He'd loved the ocean once, had made a weekly trek to some of Victoria's best surf beaches all within an hour's drive from the Central Business District. However, since starting work at Vance Corp he'd been too busy proving himself, putting in the hours, to chill out. He wanted to be the best and it came at a price: limited down time and alienating the one guy who should've been cheering him on rather than hating him for it.

'We don't have to do the brunch thing if you don't want to,' Ariel said, a tiny frown puckering her forehead as she searched his face for reassurance. 'I've got what I needed to finish the portrait so you're obligation-free now.'

'Let's eat.'

It wasn't her fault his mood had soured courtesy of thoughts of his dad's hang-ups. Besides, he wanted to make sure this final session ended on a happy note considering the next time they met he'd be pitching his plans for the gallery.

'As long as it's not my head you're biting off,' she said, sending him a knowing glance that said she hadn't bought his abrupt brush-off for a second.

'I promise to be nice.'

He led the way to the closest table, which happened to be a purple, kidney-shaped one boasting lemon vinyl chairs and a cartoon-like backdrop. Like everything else in this street, the Hideout café was bright, out there and eclectic.

Ariel fit right in with her denim shorts, indigo silk camisole top and rope espadrilles, whereas he stuck out like a beacon in his conservative navy cargo pants and white T-shirt.

Then again, he'd never fit in around here. Orange leather chaps just weren't his thing.

'See anything you fancy?'

To his amazement, Ariel blushed and toyed with a long blonde curl that persistently bounced in the vicinity of her right ear.

'I'll have the mushroom omelette.'

'And let me guess. A skinny decaf soy latte chaser?'

She tilted her nose in the air and sent him an imperious look. 'Ha! You don't know me at all. I'll have a wheatgrass, orange and ginger juice, please.'

The thought of all those ingredients blended together made him want to forgo the big fry-up he was about to order. 'Anyone ever tell you you're a health freak?'

Rather than bristling as he'd expected, she leaned back against the vinyl booth and chuckled. 'I'd rather be a health freak than any other kind of freak.'

'You are one interesting woman, Ariel Wallace,' he said, locking eyes with her over his menu, wondering if she noticed the growing attraction sizzling between them or it had just been too damn long since he'd dated.

He'd been so busy lately trying to get out of Vance Corporation that he'd neglected his social life. Once this deal went through, he'd make sure he remedied that. Though somehow, he had a feeling he'd need quite a few dates with women the antithesis of Ariel to make him forget her.

'Oh, yeah, that's me and I know exactly what you find so interesting about me.'

She quirked an eyebrow, full of sass and challenge and he wondered if he was slipping. Surely his interest in her beauty, her feisty nature, her sharp wit and her stunning body wasn't that transparent?

He settled for a safe 'What's that?' rather than make a complete fool of himself.

More than he had already, that was.

She snapped her fingers. 'My gallery, of course. We both know there's no other reason why a guy like you is hanging around a girl like me.'

She spoke calmly, without rancour, as if stating an obvious fact. The intriguing part was, even though he agreed with her, it still rankled.

'You're really into the whole stereotyping thing, aren't you?'

She shrugged. 'I'm just being honest. No use pretending when we're both grown up and we know what this is all about.'

Her hand waved between them, a smooth, flowing, graceful movement demonstrating her artistic side.

He loved watching her hands, so full of life and energy and creativity.

'You and I have a business arrangement, Cooper. You've fulfilled your part of the bargain and I'll follow through with mine. So let's just call it what it is and you can save the sweet talk. I'm going to stick to my end of the bargain whether you find me "interesting" or not.'

'You don't get compliments very often, do you?'

Which he found incredibly hard to believe considering she was a knockout.

Her green eyes narrowed, as if trying to ascertain if he was serious or toying with her.

'Dressed like this and with hair like this?' She plucked at her trendily creased top and loose curls, which hung halfway down her back in a frizzy curtain. 'What do you think?'

In response, he leaned forward and captured one of those lively, bouncy curls between his thumb and forefinger, rubbing the silky softness between them. 'I think you underestimate yourself. I also think you're beautiful.'

For one long, loaded moment she stared at him, her eyes glowing with gratitude and something more, something akin to desire, with a small, secretive smile dancing across her lips.

He tugged gently on her curl, leaning forward,

knowing what he wanted to do was crazy but unable to stop the gravitational pull towards her.

He wanted to drag her across the table, wrap his arms around her and kiss her senseless, to taste her rosy lips, to silence her sassy mouth for two seconds and see if his spiralling desire was a figment of his imagination or not.

He didn't think about business or what kissing her could do to his chances for a fair hearing.

He didn't think about tomorrow.

Instead, caught up in the moment, he leaned forward till their faces almost touched, which was exactly when Ariel placed her hand square in the middle of his chest and shoved hard, just as she'd pushed him out the door when she'd first learned his true identity.

'That isn't going to win you any Brownie points. I said I'll hear you out and I will.'

Ariel acted cool but her fiddling hands told him otherwise as they moved from pushing back her hair to adjusting her top to rearranging the cutlery.

Trying to get his ragged breathing under control, he schooled his face into a polite mask, thankful that one of them had kept their cool and furious it hadn't been him.

He needed to wrap this up and fast.

He had no room in his life for emotions.

Yet the more time he spent in Ariel's intoxicating company, he floundered and, worse, found himself re-evaluating his vows not to get close to anyone.

He had to focus on business.

It was the only way.

'I don't need to score Brownie points. My proposal will speak for itself.'

He folded his arms and determinedly avoided looking at her mouth, the very same sexy mouth he'd almost kissed a second ago.

'We'll see, Mr Big-Shot. We'll see.'

With an enigmatic smile, she called the waitress over and left him mulling over the wisdom of consorting with the enemy.

Even an enemy as delightful as Ariel.

Ariel's heart sank as she caught sight of Sofia peering through the gallery's front windows. If the verbose woman caught sight of her with Cooper, goodness knew what might pop out of her gargantuan mouth.

'Who's that?' Cooper said, his long strides making her wish she'd worn flat shoes rather than wedge-heeled espadrilles today. She felt like a munchkin running on triple speed to keep up with a giant.

'Sofia Montessori. She's the one who commissioned the portrait.'

'I thought she looked familiar. I've seen her in passing at several events.'

That'd be right. She should've known a man like Cooper would move in the same moneyed circles as Sofia.

Her feet dragged, walking at a snail's pace as they neared the front of the gallery, not wanting to get caught up in any name-dropping, name-swapping game that might take place. She hated that sort of thing, which was why she hid out in her studio and produced art for people like Sofia and Cooper rather than attend their hob-nob parties and exhibitions.

She'd been to the occasional party in her early days and hated every minute of it: the yawning cultural and social gap between her and other people, the patronising, condescending attitudes when they discovered she was the artist.

'Hurry up. She looks ready to break your door down,' Cooper said, sending her a quizzical look.

'Thanks for walking me back to the gallery but I'm fine, I'll take it from here,' she blurted, anxious to get rid of him, knowing that any second Sofia would turn her beady gaze their way and have them halfway up the aisle before she could say, 'In your dreams'.

That stopped him dead in his tracks.

'Don't you want me to meet your friend? Are you that ashamed to be seen with me?'

If Cooper's warm, friendly persona had scared her, the icy contempt she now heard in his voice terrified her more.

'It's not that. I just want to finish the portrait ASAP and if Sofia lays eyes on you, believe me she won't leave in a hurry.'

He must've been satisfied with her answer for the cold gleam in his eyes softened. 'I won't stay. Besides, I've handled worse than Sofia in the business arena and come out unscathed. Trust me.'

Shaking her head, she fell into step beside him again. The guy was seriously delusional if he thought she'd trust him with anything. He was here to tear her life apart and all the sexy smiles and almost-kisses in the world wouldn't change that.

'Sofia, what are you doing here?'

Ariel injected warmth into her voice, knowing she would've been glad to see the lovely Italian woman if Cooper's large, looming presence weren't at her side.

Sofia stopped peering through the gallery windows

and turned, and Ariel knew the exact moment she spotted them. The woman's eyes fairly bulged out of her immaculately coiffed head.

'*Ciao, bella.*' Sofia kissed both her cheeks briefly before pulling away to study Cooper with blatant curiosity, a hungry look on her expertly made-up face. 'And who is your friend? He looks awfully familiar.'

Ariel took a deep breath to perform the introductions, wishing everyone would go away and leave her alone so she could get on with the business of finishing the portrait, obtaining the money and securing the gallery for another month or so.

'Sofia, this is Cooper Vance. Cooper, my friend Sofia Montessori.'

'A pleasure, Ms Montessori.'

Cooper captured Sofia's hand and bowed over it in an antiquated gesture from years gone by. The old smoothie…

He must've known exactly how a woman like Sofia would react. She preened and simpered and practically fell in a swooning heap at his feet.

'Ditto, Mr Vance,' Sofia tittered, smiling and gushing like a teenager. 'Have we met before? I'm positive I've seen you before.'

Ariel rolled her eyes, resisting the urge to stick two fingers down her throat and make gagging noises.

'Your reputation in Melbourne society precedes you. Perhaps we've seen each other in passing at a function?'

Sofia's eyes narrowed, her gaze speculative. 'No, I don't think so. It's somewhere more recent…'

'Would you like a cup of coffee, Sofia? Cooper was just leaving and I really have lots of work to do.'

Ariel didn't want Sofia connecting Cooper to the portrait right now. If that happened…

'That's it! You're the model in my portrait.' Sofia's hungry gaze travelled the length of Cooper's body while Ariel's heart sank.

Great, just great.

'*Bello*,' Sofia murmured, obviously liking what she saw.

Not that Ariel could blame her. Sofia was a red-blooded woman after all and if she'd admired Ariel's sketches of the man, they were nothing on the real, live model in the flesh. So to speak.

Cooper smiled, a brash, unaffected smile that made Ariel want to throttle him for being so blasé about the whole situation. 'Yes, I'm sitting for Ariel. She's a very talented artist. I think you'll be very pleased with the final result.'

'And a nice boy, too,' Sofia said, sending Ariel a pointed look as if to say, Are you crazy to let this guy get away? Why aren't you married by now and expecting his *bambino*?

'Speaking of which, I better finish the portrait if you want it by Tuesday—'

'You must come too, Mr Vance!' Sofia's loud voice drowned out a passing tram as she waved her hands about in excitement. 'Ariel is coming to the little soirée I'm having for my sister's birthday where the portrait will be unveiled and it is only natural that you should attend also.'

'No!' Ariel blurted out before she could stop herself, blushing furiously when two sets of eyes turned on her, Sofia's knowing brown eyes and Cooper's dazzling blue.

'I mean, I'm sure Cooper has better things to do with his time. Besides, he'd probably be mortified if people recognise him as the model. He's a businessman and it wouldn't look good at all.'

Ariel babbled on and on, sending Cooper the evil eye, silently praying he'd back her up on this.

She didn't want him anywhere near that party. They'd spent enough 'social' time together, what with coffee on Friday night and brunch today. The longer she spent with him, the more befuddled she became and she needed her wits about her to fob him off after listening to his stupid proposal.

Liking someone, enjoying their company, wasn't conducive to kicking them out the door, and that was exactly what she'd have to do after hearing his pitch.

So no more social stuff.

Starting now.

'What do you think, Mr Vance?'

Sofia frowned at Ariel before turning on a charming smile for Cooper.

'I think it's a great idea. Thanks for the invitation.'

'*Bene*! That's all settled. Now, why don't we go in and I can give you all the details?'

Ignoring Sofia's triumphant expression and Cooper's smug smile, Ariel sighed in resignation and unlocked the front door.

Two against one wasn't fair.

But then, since when had anything in her life been fair?

CHAPTER EIGHT

'I SHOULD never have agreed to this,' Ariel muttered at her reflection, wishing she could wield a mascara wand with the same expertise as a paintbrush.

She'd never gone in for the whole make up thing. She much preferred painting canvases to painting her face. Then again, tonight called for a confidence mask and if the barest foundation, sheer blue eye-shadow, a quick lashing of mascara and pale pink lip gloss would help quell the butterflies dancing a tango in her belly, she'd use it.

Seeing Cooper at Sofia's charity event was one thing, but agreeing to go with him?

Madness.

Right on cue, a sharp knock at the front door had her casting one last regretful look at her reflection in the mirror before she picked up her embroidered silver evening purse and flicked off the lights.

Though how hard could tonight be?

She'd wait around till the portrait was unveiled, make polite small talk with a bunch of rich phoneys then bolt back here in a taxi, leaving Cooper with his cronies.

Easy.

However, the minute she opened the door and saw Cooper standing there wearing a designer tux and a sexy smile, she knew nothing about this evening would be easy.

In fact, the way her pulse accelerated and her heart flip-flopped, nothing could be further from the truth.

'Wow, you look beautiful.'

He stepped into the doorway, blocking out the night sounds of a busy Brunswick Street, and took hold of her hand. His voice was soft, almost reverent, like a gentle caress and she shivered with delight that she could evoke a reaction like that from a guy like him.

'It's vintage,' she said, a totally inane remark. She stood frozen to the spot, her hand captured in his, enjoying the physical contact way too much.

As if he was interested in her dress.

'It suits you.'

Finally, after the hand-holding had gone on too long, he released her hand only to skim his palm over the sheer chiffon cascading in handkerchief layers from her waist to the floor.

'You look like a beautiful waterfall. Fresh, vibrant, invigorating.'

'And you need to move into the twenty-first century. With lines like that, I'm not surprised you spend all your time with your head buried behind a computer.'

She didn't mean to sound so cutting but she didn't handle compliments well. Especially compliments from a guy standing way too close and smelling like a dream come true.

To her surprise, he laughed rather than rebuke her. 'You're not going to spoil tonight with that smart mouth of yours. Insult me all you like but I'm not biting.'

More's the pity.

He raised an eyebrow as if reading her mind and she propelled him out the door, anything to put some much needed distance between them. Even seated in his car would be better than having him invade her personal space. Not that she minded exactly but if they didn't get a move on she'd be tempted to rush back into the gallery, slip back into shorts and a poncho and have a TV dinner while watching her favourite DIY house-renovation show.

Boring but safe.

The complete antithesis of allowing Cooper to drape her hand in the crook of his elbow and lead her to his low-slung sports car parked around the corner.

Exciting and dangerous.

Yeah, that was Cooper through and through. For a girl who liked being dull and safe she sure was tempted by the prospect of living a little for once.

'Flash wheels,' she said, sliding into the plush leather interior as he held the passenger door open for her.

'It was a present.'

She looked at him in surprise, his abrupt tone implying he didn't like it. Or maybe didn't like the person who had given it to him?

As he slid behind the wheel, started the engine and pulled away from the kerb, she couldn't resist probing further. 'Let me guess. Daddy bought it for you as a bonus last year?'

'Close,' he said, his voice tight, his hands clenched around the steering wheel.

She could've left it there but she didn't. After being virtually ignored for the first eight years of her life as she'd flitted from orphanage to foster home and back again, living with Barb had opened a whole new world to her. Barb had encouraged her natural curiosity, had answered her endless questions with the patience of a saint.

Ariel loved mystery novels for that very reason, always wanting questions answered, the unsolvable unravelled and, right now, she had a doozy of a puzzle laid out before her and there was no way she could back down.

'Pretty generous gift. You two must be close.'

'We were.'

Okay, maybe now was the time to keep her mouth shut. Cooper's use of past tense could only mean two things; they'd fallen out or, worse, his father was dead.

'We don't get along these days,' Cooper said, his icy tone sending chills down her spine.

'I'm sorry.'

And she was, for ever thinking she could make tonight work. Even when she was trying to fit in, she made a mess of things. Rather than keeping the conversation light, she'd had to push, nosing around where she didn't belong.

Great.

'So am I.'

Cooper didn't say any more and this time she didn't push, clamping her glossed lips tightly shut and staring out the window at the glittering lights of Melbourne as they wound their way to Toorak, one of the city's richest suburbs.

However, after five minutes passed and the uncomfortable silence yawned between them, she said, 'Do you have any music?'

'Sure.'

He fiddled with a few chrome buttons that looked as

if they could launch the space shuttle until muted jazz filled the car.

'How's that?'

'Not bad,' she said, hoping for something more upbeat. Anything to lighten the mood.

'What sort of music do you like?'

'Latin American. Flamenco. Anything with a bit of oomph.'

And the exact opposite of his choice, but she wisely kept that tidbit to herself.

However, he zoned in on her thoughts with unerring accuracy once again.

'You think I'm some kind of business-oriented bore, don't you?'

Got it in one, Coop!

However, in the interests of making the rest of the drive and the hour or so of torture she had ahead of her at the party bearable, she chose her words carefully.

'We're different, that's all.'

'Like opposites attract and all that?'

'Who said anything about attraction?'

She kept her tone deliberately light, knowing she'd successfully stepped through one verbal minefield only to plough straight into another.

A more dangerous minefield this time, one with the potential to detonate and leave her heart in tiny, shattered fragments if she acknowledged her growing attraction to this guy.

'Come on, you can tell me the truth. I've seen how you look at me when you're painting.'

'What a load of—'

His laughter drowned out the rest of her response and

she reluctantly joined in, recognising she'd been had and how he'd effectively lightened the mood.

'Okay, now I can add enormous ego to the list of your faults, you better quit while you're behind.'

'Ah…so you're fixated on my behind too, huh?'

Sending him a glare that could melt wax, she was unprepared for the swift, scorching glance he fired right back at her.

Thankfully, they were stopped at traffic lights otherwise the heat they created with that one locked stare would've made the engine seize or made him ram a light pole, whichever came first.

Tilting her nose in the air and sending him a superior smile, she said, 'The way I observed your body was purely professional. Anything else you imagine you saw is pure speculation on your part. Incorrect speculation I might add.'

He chuckled and refocussed on the road as the lights changed to green, his deep, rich laughter rolling over her like low-lying clouds on a sultry summer's day. 'Come on, Ariel, admit it. You want my body.'

'I want your head on a platter, preferably with an apple stuffed in that big mouth of yours.'

To her annoyance, heat crawled under her skin, setting her nerve endings alight with longing.

He was right, darn it.

She did want his body.

The whole look-but-don't-touch thing had driven her slowly but surely mad over the last week or so and the more time they spent together, the more quips they traded, the more they laughed, she knew it wasn't just his magnificent body she wanted.

She was attracted to his mind too.

The same mind that is busily hatching plots to snatch the gallery and your life away from you.

How gullible could she be?

'On that note, we're here,' he said, pulling into a long, tree-lined driveway boasting enough fancy cars to keep thieves rolling in wealth till the next century.

Men in prim black uniforms rushed about like hyperactive penguins, opening car doors, taking keys and keeping the long line of vehicles moving at a steady pace past the imposing double doors at the front of the house, thrown open to let light from a crystal chandelier spill onto the marble-tiled entry porch.

Ariel unconsciously reached for a curl to twist around her finger, forgetting she'd piled most of them on top of her head in a poor imitation of a posh up-do.

This place wasn't her.

From the ostentatious cream-rendered, double-storey house that sprawled across the large block, the flood-lit tennis court she glimpsed behind the house to the right and the hand-trimmed topiary trees that looked like a real, live zoo leading up to the entrance, every self-preserving instinct told Ariel to make a run for it now.

People who lived in places like this, who drove cars like the ones lining the drive, who attended parties like this, meant one thing to her.

Trouble.

She'd battled the prejudices of rich people her entire life and, despite how far she'd come, she hated the feelings they evoked as they looked down their aristocratic noses at the scruffy, weird artist as if she hadn't risen far enough out of the gutter.

She didn't think she had a hang-up about her past, but whenever she got within two feet of a patronising snob all her old insecurities rushed back and left her feeling inadequate.

'What's wrong?'

Cooper had put the car into park mode and turned to face her, a frown lining his forehead.

'This isn't my scene.'

Her hand fluttered to her face again, searching for that elusive curl to twirl in comfort and coming up empty again.

Great, the one time that lousy curl behaved itself and actually stayed tucked up and off her face she had the urge to rip it down and twist it around and around her finger.

'Consider it part of your job,' he said, his voice soft and soothing. 'This is networking at its best, where you get to scope out potential customers, feed them what they want to hear, promote your business. And if all else fails, fall back on the old standard.'

'What's that?'

'Picture the lot of them naked.'

She managed a tight smile, suddenly grateful for his presence and the support he was offering. It would've been so much harder to walk in there alone. With Cooper, one of their own, she could blend into the background without too much difficulty.

'Anyone ever tell you you've got a fixation on the naked human form?'

'That's you, sweetheart, not me.'

He reached out and squeezed her hand, a brief, impersonal touch but supportive nonetheless and she could've kissed him for it.

Though she wouldn't go there…not if she knew what was good for her.

'Ready to go in?'

'Ready as I'll ever be,' she muttered, tugging on her tight bodice and patting the top of her head tentatively to see if her thick, unmanageable mop was still in place.

'Remember, think naked,' he said, giving her a heart-stopping smile before releasing her hand and stepping out of the car.

'It's show-time,' she murmured, feeling more like a bit actress than the star attraction and hoping she wouldn't fluff her lines.

Ironically, it wasn't only the hoity-toity crowd who had her stomach rolling with nerves but the thought she might make a fool of herself with Cooper, whose opinion she'd come to care way too much about.

Silly, irrational, absurd, and the sooner tonight was over, he delivered his pitch and he exited her life, the better off she'd be.

Then why the scary, empty feeling at the thought?

Cooper stuck to Ariel's side for several reasons: she looked stunning and he wanted to protect her from every man in the room, she'd seemed scared and vulnerable in the car and, lastly but most importantly, he wanted her next to him for the purely selfish reason that he liked having her there.

The quirky, sassy woman had him laughing more than he had in ages and he enjoyed firing right back at her. Not to mention the way her unique green eyes sparkled with glee when she scored a direct hit with her teasing barbs.

However, spending time with Ariel had one major drawback: he had to keep reminding himself of the real reason, the only reason, he was with her.

Business.

He'd never lost sight of the ultimate goal in any deal and he wouldn't start now. Not when leaving Vance Corporation was so important. Correction, when it was vital.

He'd had it with his dad. Time to get away, start up a little healthy competition and see if that made the old man sit up and take notice.

'Oh-oh, look at all these people.'

Ariel gripped his arm tighter and all but yanked him behind a marble pillar as they stepped into an elaborate foyer.

'Hey, wasn't my pep talk in the car worth anything?' He refrained from patting her hand, knowing she'd probably sock him straight in the nose for it.

She shook her head vigorously and the pile of curls on top wobbled, enveloping him in a bizarre fruity-floral scent he'd yet to identify and was too embarrassed to ask her about. The same scent that haunted him, enticed him and beckoned him to get closer to her.

'Sorry, the whole naked visualisation thing doesn't do it for me.'

'Even after seeing me with my clothes off?'

She rolled her eyes but at least he saw a glimmer of a smile.

'Especially after that!'

'Ouch, you sure know how to wound a guy's ego.'

He clutched his heart in mock pain, eliciting more of a smile from her enticing mouth coated in a shiny gloss.

He'd never seen her wear make up before. Her subtle use of cosmetics tonight just highlighted her exquisite features.

'With an ego the size of yours, Mr Big-Shot, I seriously doubt that.'

Shaking his head and exceedingly pleased his distraction technique had worked, he said, 'I take it the whole Mr Big-Shot isn't a term of endearment?'

Her smile faded. 'It's a fact. You're a big shot, I'm an artist. You want something I have, which is the only reason you're here tonight and being so darn nice to me. So let's go in, do the obligatory social thing and get out of here before this Cinderella turns into a pumpkin.'

'Fine,' he muttered, not sure if he was more annoyed by how little she thought of him or by the element of truth behind her brutal honesty.

'Fine,' she said, tilting her head up like a queen and marching away, leaving him with a tantalising view of a straight, bare back courtesy of her daring dress. The rest of it cascaded from her waist to the floor in shimmery shades of aquamarine, turquoise and emerald, the exact colour of the Great Barrier Reef on a clear day.

The woman was a burr in his side.

He tried to be nice and what did he get for his trouble? An earful.

He tried to be rational about this whole business deal between them and what did he get? Angst.

And she hadn't even heard his pitch yet.

Okay, so maybe he was the heartless tycoon she thought he was. He'd never pretended otherwise.

Business meant everything to him.

It was all he knew.

He'd blitzed his degrees, waltzed into a job and proceeded to set the business world alight. He deserved to be confident. Failure wasn't in his vocabulary. Never had been, never would be.

And no matter how stubborn the eccentric Miss Wallace wanted to be, he'd make sure he wouldn't fail this time.

He couldn't. There was too much at stake.

'You are enjoying yourself, *bella*, yes?'

Ariel took a sip of her sparkling mineral water, not wanting to lie to Sofia and needing a few seconds to compose an honest but graceful answer.

'Everyone seems to be having a wonderful time,' Ariel said, knowing it sounded lame and the astute Sofia would pick up on it in a second.

She did.

'I do not care for everyone else, *bella*. What about you? Is everything all right?'

Ariel nodded and forced a smile, hoping it didn't look like a grimace. 'Guess I'm just tired after rushing the portrait.'

Sofia's expertly made up face beamed. 'Ah...yes, the portrait. It is *magnifico*! Maria loves it.'

'And seems to be infatuated with the model.'

Ariel inclined her head towards Sofia's sister, who for a woman of forty looked fifteen years younger in a siren-red poured-on dress, luscious dark hair that hung in perfect waves to her shoulders and huge, expressive brown eyes that were firmly fixed on Cooper, along with her talon-like hands gripping his arm as she stared up at him.

'So that's it...' Sofia waved her hand towards Maria

in an abrupt, dismissive gesture. 'Don't be jealous, *bella;* she is no competition to you.'

Ariel stiffened, not liking Sofia's implication. She wasn't jealous. She'd have to care to be jealous and she didn't. Caring about Cooper would be like skipping into the dentist with a big, goofy grin on her face and clapping her hands with glee: pure and utter madness.

'I'm not interested in Cooper so you can get that maniacal matchmaking gleam out of your eyes,' Ariel said, sending Sofia a forceful look that meant business.

Predictably, the Italian woman ignored her. 'How can you not be interested? The man is beautiful, successful, charming, cultured—'

'And out to ruin me.'

Ariel glared at Cooper through narrow eyes, wondering why he let himself be pawed. Didn't the guy have any dignity?

Considering how fast he'd whipped off his clothes to insinuate his way into her good books, probably not.

'Maybe you should listen to him, see what he has to say about the gallery before jumping to conclusions?'

Sofia's tone had softened and Ariel knew that, though she meant well, in this case her friend didn't have a clue.

'That so-called charming man probably wants to kick me out of the gallery, tear it down and erect some awful monstrosity that won't fit in with Brunswick Street. I've been fobbing off his kind ever since Aunt Barb died. He's not the first and he won't be the last. The one thing I'm sure of, I'm not leaving. I promised Aunt Barb.'

Sofia laid a comforting hand on her arm, patting it gently. 'Babs would've wanted you to be happy. She was one of my closest friends and I know how much she loved you, how much joy you brought to her life. She would want the same for you. Instead, you're working too hard, battling too hard to keep the place open. You won't accept help from anyone and you bristle like some feral cat whenever anyone offers. Perhaps it is time to reconsider, *bella*?'

'No!'

Sofia jumped, the concern in her dark eyes hardening Ariel's resolve.

She didn't want to reconsider anything.

She'd made a promise to Aunt Barb and she'd do her best to keep it. She had to.

All she'd had to offer Aunt Barb in return for years of unswerving love and support was her word and there was no way she would break this promise even if it meant taking on ten extra jobs. Or doing ten more life portraits—as much as she hated them.

Though if all the models looked like Cooper…

Mentally slapping herself for going there, she enveloped Sofia in a hug. 'I'm sorry for biting your head off. I know you mean well, but I have to do this my own way.'

Sofia pulled back and patted her cheek. 'In that case, why don't you go and mingle? Several people have expressed interest in getting portraits done by the fabulous artist who painted Maria's birthday present. And, of course, the men are all dying to meet the gorgeous creature in the stunning green dress.'

Ariel glanced down at the fitted bodice, spaghetti straps and pointy-panelled, flowing chiffon of her vintage dress. With all the couture in this room, they thought this dress was stunning? Just proved her point about what a bunch of phoneys this rich crowd was.

However, obtaining a few more commissions could mean the difference between staying open for another year or not and, though she hated the patronising, condescending atmosphere in the room, she'd swallow her pride and think of Colour by Dreams.

'You're not pushing them in my direction, I hope?'

Sofia threw her hands up in theatrical despair. '*Bella*, how could you think such a thing?'

She winked and gave Ariel a none-too-gentle shove towards the main throng gathered at the floor-to-ceiling French doors opening out onto a sandstone-paved patio. 'Now go!'

'I'm going, I'm going,' Ariel muttered, downing the rest of her mineral water and suddenly wishing she liked the taste of champagne. A little false courage wouldn't have gone astray at this point considering she hated marketing, particularly self-promotion.

Not surprising, when she'd spent the first eight years of her life trying to fade into the background at the various orphanages, foster homes and during that interminable week-long stint on the streets.

Falling asleep in an old canvas in Barb's backyard had been the luckiest break of her life. Now, if only her luck could hold...like for the next twenty years or so.

'Going somewhere?'

A hand clamped on her arm out of nowhere and she stopped, shrugging off Cooper's grip before speaking.

'I'm off to do some networking, just as some business guru advised me on the way over here.'

Cooper smiled and she wished her heart wouldn't do

that weird little tango whenever he did. 'You mean you're actually listening to me? And, better yet, taking my advice?'

'Yeah, go figure? I must be drunk.'

'On that clear sparkling stuff you've been drinking for the last hour? I doubt it.'

A small part of Ariel was flattered that he'd managed to tear his gaze away from fawning Maria for more than a second to notice what she'd been drinking while a larger part—the logical part—told her she was crazy for caring.

'Look, why don't you head back to your friends and let me continue doing what I have to do?' *And the only reason why I came here in the first place.* 'In fact, once I finish chatting to a few people I'll never see again if I'm lucky, I'm heading home, so thanks for the lift.'

His smile vanished and his eyes darkened to a stormy midnight. 'Firstly, these people aren't my friends. They're acquaintances and the main reason I'm here is to support you, not party with people I barely know. Secondly, I'm not some immature little boy you can give the brush-off to when it suits you. I brought you, I'll take you home. And lastly, in case you didn't know, this whole "woe-is-me" act of yours is wearing a little thin. You're out of your depth here? Well, listen up, sweetheart. Everyone gets that feeling, from the Prime Minister to garbage collectors. You're a big girl, deal with it. Now off you go, show these people half the spunk you show me, and when you're ready I'll meet you outside.'

Ariel stared at Cooper in stunned disbelief as he strode through the open French doors without looking back, torn between wanting to run after him and give him a clip around the ears for speaking to her like that and doing exactly as he said: going out there and making this crowd notice her, make some contacts, promoting her business, no matter how much she hated it and how far out of her depth she felt.

Woe-is-me?

'I'll show him,' she muttered, glaring daggers in the general direction of the patio and squaring her shoulders to do what she had to do.

'You do know the only reason I let you drive me home was because I couldn't get a taxi for over an hour?'

Ariel flounced ahead of Cooper into the studio, not bothering to turn on more lights than the two corner elephant lamps she'd picked up for a song at a local car-boot sale.

He wouldn't be here long enough. Once she'd set a time for him to deliver his almighty proposal, she'd kick him out the door and concentrate on sorting through the business cards that had been discreetly palmed her way this evening.

Sofia had been right. People were interested in her work. Though, realistically, even if she worked night and day for the next few months, the commissions wouldn't stave off the inevitable.

She needed money, a lot of it, to keep the gallery running and, right now, with Cooper staring at her with a speculative gleam in his too-blue eyes, reminding her exactly why he was here, she knew she was fast running out of options.

'Well, I didn't think it was for my scintillating company, considering you didn't speak and pouted the whole way.'

'I didn't pout!'

'No? Then what's that pursing-up thing you're doing with your lips right now?'

Before she could blink, Cooper leaned forward, his thumb gently brushing across her lips and setting up a delicious tingle that spread throughout her body, lingering in places that hadn't tingled in a long while.

'Nothing to say? That's a first.'

Ariel couldn't have spoken if she'd wanted to. Her tongue was glued to the roof of her mouth at the sheer shock of being touched by Cooper like this, as if he wanted her, as if she were more than the enemy to him.

Besides, she was too scared to speak. If she opened her mouth, there was no telling what she might do with his thumb in the vicinity of her mouth, when her main impulse was to nibble it.

His thumb skidded across her bottom lip and drifted lower, tracing a slow, leisurely path along her jaw and back, making her knees wobble and her body sway towards him with a will of its own.

'Guess I better go before you ply me with any of your herbal concoctions, huh?'

He cupped her cheek, his hypnotic stare mesmerising, as if the last thing he wanted to do was leave.

Or was that her interpretation of it?

Was she wishing for something that wasn't there, considering he made her feel like *this*?

Like a desirable woman, like an equal, like someone he admired?

When he touched her like this, looked at her like this, she could almost forget the huge, yawning gap between them, a gap that attending the party tonight only reinforced.

Cooper belonged in the rich, uppity crowd she would've shunned given half a chance; she didn't. Never had, never would and that was just fine by her. He knew it, she knew it, then what was this tender act about?

Suddenly, it hit her.

The proposal.

The type of guy he was: a cold, arrogant businessman, who would probably do anything to get what he wanted.

However, before she could shove him away, he dropped his hand and stepped back, regret etched across his striking face.

'Mind telling me what that was all about?'

She tilted her head back to stare him in the eye, challenging, needing an answer and knowing it was futile to hope it wasn't what she suspected.

'I think you know,' he said, his gaze travelling over her from head to foot, slowly, lingering, and making her body shudder with need as if his hands had skimmed a similar trail. 'But until you're willing to admit it even exists, I'm not going to do anything about this attraction between us. And, no, it has nothing to do with business and everything to do with you and me and the way you drive me crazy.'

And for the second time that night, she allowed Cooper to walk away from her, leaving her gob-smacked.

CHAPTER NINE

COOPER finished reading the last page of the proposal, returned it to the stack of papers in front of him and tidied up the lot before slipping the copy into a presentation folder.

This was it.

D-day.

Developer day, when he convinced Ariel to sign over the gallery, guaranteeing him a new start away from his cantankerous old man.

The documentation was flawless and he'd planned for every contingency.

Apart from the one where she said no to his immaculately laid-out plans.

Though that wouldn't happen if she knew what was good for her. After getting to know the bohemian beauty, he knew for a fact that Ariel's brain was as impressive as the rest of her.

Something his father would've recognised if he hadn't barged into this deal with all the finesse of a wounded rhino. Then again, his dad hadn't even rated Ariel, preferring to deal through the council that held her lease.

A small part of Cooper wished his dad had sealed this deal because that would've given him free rein to pursue Ariel, to explore the sizzling attraction between them, to kiss her…

Damn, he'd been so tempted last night, so close to throwing his ideals to the wind, hauling her into his arms and making every fantasy he'd ever had about her come true. Thankfully, his befuddled brain had kicked into gear at the last minute and he'd averted a mini disaster.

As much as he wanted Ariel, he wanted to get out of Vance Corporation more and make his stubborn old coot of a dad wake up.

'Got a minute?'

Speak of the devil…

Eric strode into the office without waiting for an invite and stood over Cooper's desk.

'Sure, what's up?'

It irked Cooper that he couldn't call Eric 'Dad' in the office. In fact, they'd both dropped the 'dad and son' act as soon as he'd joined the company. Sad but true.

He'd tried damn hard, putting in long hours, nailing big deals, doing more for Vance Corporation than any other employee in history.

No more.

'What's the deal with the Wallace woman? You signed her yet? We're due to meet with the investors in a few days.'

Cooper tapped the document folder in front of him. 'I'm meeting with her in an hour.'

An ugly sneer creased Eric's face. 'Well, that's just dandy but is she going to sign on the dotted line?'

'I'm confident.'

Cooper kept his answers short, non-confrontational, just as he'd learned to do in view of his dad's ever-increasing short temper.

'What then?'

Cooper stared at his dad in confusion. They'd never talked beyond the deal. Cooper knew the day he delivered the signed documentation was the day he walked out of here with his contract in tatters but his dad had never asked about his future plans. He just wasn't interested.

'Do you really want to know?'

To his surprise, Eric slumped into the chair opposite and lost the surly expression.

'Yeah, I do. You've worked here ever since uni; guess I'm entitled to know your plans.'

'As my ex-employer or as my father?'

Cooper almost spat the words even though he knew now wasn't the time or place to have the whole in-depth father/son chat he'd wanted for the last year.

He had more important things to focus on—like convincing a crazy artist to hand over her studio.

'I deserved that.'

If Cooper had been surprised by his dad's question, Eric's concerned expression floored him.

For a moment, it almost looked as if his dad cared.

'Look, Coop, things have been pretty full-on around here for the last year. Maybe I've taken you for granted. You're a good worker. You'll go places. Seems a shame to throw it all away on a whim.'

Cooper's tiny flicker of hope was extinguished in that second.

His dad wasn't interested in re-establishing a

father/son bond. His dad was only concerned about his precious business.

He should've known.

Cooper stood up abruptly, shrugged into his suit jacket and picked up the presentation folder. 'Thanks for the vote of confidence, but this isn't a whim. Striking out on my own is something I have to do. You'd understand that if you knew me.'

Cooper ignored the stricken look in his father's eyes and walked out the door, his attention already focussed on the meeting ahead and its importance for his future.

Ariel fussed around the studio, lighting her lime and tangerine candles, plumping the sequinned purple cushions on the ruby sofas and tidying up the evidence of her nerves.

She'd drunk about a dozen cups of chamomile tea since ringing Cooper this morning and telling him today was as good a time as any to hear his pitch and now, as she stacked the cups in the dishwasher and made her umpteenth bolt for the loo, she wondered if she'd done the right thing.

'Keep your friends close and your enemies closer' had been one of Barb's favourite sayings so Ariel had taken the plunge and rung him, despite her tummy still churning since their almost-kiss last night.

If she'd had her way, she would've never laid eyes on the too-gorgeous guy again but they'd made a deal, he'd upheld his end of the bargain and now it was her turn.

As she glanced around the studio her heart swelled with pride. Sunlight streamed through the soaring windows, filtered through the colourful gauze swaths of chiffon she'd hung from curtain hooks, casting a warm, rainbow-like feel over the room. Combined with the refreshing tang of citrus from the aromatherapy candles and the bright ruby and amethyst colour combination of the furniture against the polished oak boards, the place looked inviting: warm, welcoming, a haven.

And it was her haven. Had been from the minute she'd set foot into this room, a scared and starving eight-year-old who'd thought she'd stepped into Aladdin's treasure cave.

She wanted Cooper to see the studio how she saw it, to feel its ambience, to recognise how much it meant to her.

This wasn't just about her fervent promise to Aunt Barb. This was her home, the only home she'd ever had and she would fight with everything she had to hold onto it.

The wind chimes over the gallery front door tinkled and Ariel took a deep breath, wondering if she was more nervous about rejecting Cooper's pitch or seeing the guy so soon after he'd almost made her swoon like the women of her past whose vintage styles she favoured.

'Ariel?'

'Be right there,' she called out, casting one last frantic gaze around the studio and wondering if it was too late to wear her lucky garland.

Though it would clash terribly with her flowing, flower-child dress cinched at the waist with a crocheted macramé belt, and pink flip-flops. Not that she usually cared, revelling in combining colours, patterns, fabrics and shoes with creative abandon, but she'd already told Cooper about the garland's significance and she didn't want him prying any further.

Crossing her fingers behind her back that after hearing Cooper's pitch she wouldn't want to tear his eyes out, she pushed through the beaded curtain. 'Right on time. This business meeting must be important to you.'

'It is.'

Her tone had been light and flippant, his was anything but. Combined with his charcoal designer suit, white shirt and burgundy tie, and an expression that could've frozen ice in Antarctica, he looked ready for business. Serious business.

Ironic, considering she could've sworn he'd had monkey business on his mind when last here.

'Go through and I'll flip the lunch sign. How long is this going to take?'

'Not long if you're sensible about it.'

Ariel's narrow-eyed glare was lost as Cooper strode past her and into the studio.

She waited for some recognition of her efforts, some small comment that he appreciated the beauty of the room, but, after locking the door, flipping the sign and heading back into the studio, one look at the grim expression on his handsome face told her she'd prettied up the place for nothing.

He didn't get it.

Not that she should be surprised. Despite the cute chats, the traded barbs, the light-hearted banter they'd exchanged, Cooper was basically the cold-hearted businessman she'd labelled him as soon as as she'd learned his identity.

So he'd dulled her senses with his nice act? Looked as if he was here to well and truly pull the blinkers off today.

'Have a seat. Would you like a drink?'

'No, thanks.'

He barely looked at her, rifling through some huge, scary black folder in his hands before pulling out an equally scary huge wad of paper.

'If you're going to bamboozle me with a whole lot of facts and figures about projections and land values, forget it. Just give me the basics.'

She plopped onto one of the sofas, kicked off her flip-flops and curled her feet under her. Though her insides churned with dread, she needed to present a cool, calm façade and making herself comfortable was part of that. Maybe she should invite this new, uptight version of Cooper to slip out of his shoes and take a load off too?

She smothered a giggle at the thought.

'I'm glad to see you in such a good mood,' he said, sending her a quizzical look as he perched on the opposite end of the sofa, as far away from her physically as he could get without sliding onto the floor in an un-dignified heap.

'Let's keep it that way,' she said, pasting a confident smile on her face when in fact she desperately needed to make another mad dash to the loo.

He didn't return her smile.

In fact, he didn't do much of anything.

His face appeared carved out of granite, his blue eyes cold and flat like Port Phillip Bay on a frigid winter's day.

Darn it, she'd known he had this side to him. In fact, this was probably the real Cooper and the nice side he'd been showing her had been part of his elaborate plan to loosen her up in preparation for this day.

She'd been a fool.

But then again, what had she lost apart from a few

nights' sleep? She'd had the most amazing, erotic dreams of her life about a model with a body to die for and an artist who'd turned to sculpting and therefore had to have her hands all over him.

'You want the basics?'

'Uh-huh.'

'Okay.'

He laid down his hefty sheaf of papers on the coffee-table in front of them and turned to face her, those chilly, lifeless eyes scaring her more than the words she knew would pour out of his mouth. 'Here's how it is. This gallery is on land that is leased and that lease is coming up for renewal very shortly. Apparently, Barbara Kane, who signed the original lease, signed it for twenty-five years and in doing so effectively gave you control after she passed away. You have refused previous offers to vacate the property but, in effect, it will be in your interest to consider accepting the offer I've set out in the documentation. Otherwise, once the lease runs out, you may find you have no option but to leave with nothing as the council can re-lease or sell to anyone they please.'

Ariel stared at Cooper in growing horror, hearing every cold, callous word he uttered, wishing she didn't understand.

However, she did, all too well.

She'd known about the lease being up for renewal shortly but she'd assumed the council would be happy to renegotiate with her. After all, she was a good tenant.

She paid her rent on time—mostly.

She didn't cause trouble at all—apart from that one, tiny fire in the storeroom, which hadn't been technically her fault.

Besides, the council always supported local ventures, encouraging the alternative, hip vibe that made Brunswick Street unique. Mr Big-Shot was just trying to scare her into giving him what he wanted and she wouldn't budge.

She would continue to make Colour by Dreams one of Melbourne's most prominent galleries—if she scraped up enough money over the next few months to pay her sky-rocketing overheads—and face the lease renewal when it came up.

'By that horrified look on your face, I'm guessing you're not too keen on the idea.'

Ariel tucked her legs tighter and folded her arms, inadequate defence mechanisms against the onslaught of trouble she was facing.

'Your powers of deduction are amazing. I'm not surprised you're such a great businessman.'

'Don't!'

Cooper stood abruptly and strode to a window, his gaze fixed on some faraway spot, though what he found so intriguing about the run-down fence, the back neighbour's rusted chimney flue or the pile of old easels she'd never know.

'Don't what? Call it how it is? Throw in a little sarcasm to lighten the mood? Come on, you've had your fun, let me have mine.'

She unfolded her legs in one smooth movement and stood, joining him at the window to gaze out at the tiny square patch of backyard, the same patch she'd curled up in eighteen years earlier on that freezing winter's night when she'd been so famished, so light-headed, she hadn't been able to take another step.

'This is a business proposal. It's nothing personal,' he said, not turning to acknowledge her, not moving a muscle.

Not personal?

She could quite happily sock him in the nose for that one. Everything about this low-down deal was personal.

Taking away her home? Personal.

Ruining her dreams? Personal.

Making her break a promise to the one woman who had ever taken a chance on her? Personal.

Destroying her plans to continue Barb's work in fostering local talent and helping street kids as she'd once been? Personal, personal, personal!

Whirling to face him, she grabbed hold of his arm, forcing him to look at her. 'You just don't get it, do you? Look around. Tell me what you see.'

At least she finally got a reaction out of him, a tiny frown indenting his forehead.

'Do it!' she said, tugging on his arm when he didn't move. 'Go on, describe what you see.'

After a long pause, he turned to face the studio and she dropped her hand, determinedly ignoring the heat scorching her palm.

'Big room. Polished boards. Two red sofas. Sparkly cushions. Heap of art stuff. Fancy material which could be curtains.' His flat, deadpan voice suited his flat, deadpan description perfectly and her heart sank further.

She'd known they were worlds apart with little common ground but she'd hoped he might've developed some aesthetic sense over the last few weeks, some idea of what she was about and where she was at.

She'd been wrong.

About everything.

Including her warped, messed-up feelings that she might actually like this guy. She'd thought once she knocked back his stupid business proposal they might actually have a chance at being more than friends.

Right now even friends seemed out of the question and it hurt more than it should.

'What else do you see?' she urged, giving him one last chance to show her he understood where she was coming from, where she was going.

'Tiny kitchenette, elephant lamps, candles, art magazines.'

He turned back to her, an expectant look on his face like a pupil expecting praise from a teacher.

Praise? In his case, he'd just scored a big, fat F.

'You would see that,' she muttered, turning away from him and crossing the room so he wouldn't see the sudden tears filling her eyes.

She never cried, yet the harder she blinked them away, the more tears swelled in her eyes till they soon overflowed and ran down her cheeks in pitiful rivulets.

'I'm not sure I understand.'

Thankfully, Cooper's voice came from near the windows, indicating he hadn't moved.

She didn't want him to see her like this.

She wouldn't give him the satisfaction.

'I didn't think you would,' she murmured, holding back the sobs that threatened to join the tears. 'Just go. Leave the proposal. I'll consider it and get back to you.'

'But I need an answer—'

'I don't care what you need! Please leave and lock the door behind you.'

Her voice shook and she bit down on her bottom lip

to stop the quivering, hating him for making her feel this vulnerable, this weak.

'I'll call you,' he said, his footsteps echoing on the polished boards as he left the studio, the soft tinkling of the wind chimes an eerie signal to his departure.

'Don't bother,' she muttered, dashing an angry hand across her eyes only to find the tears falling faster than before.

Furious at Cooper, furious at her impotent tears and furious at her inability to see a clear way out of this mess, she marched into the kitchen and flicked on the kettle.

A cup of chamomile tea mightn't soothe her seething soul but it would go a long way to erasing the awful chill that had seeped into her bones at the thought she might lose this place.

And that Cooper didn't give a damn.

CHAPTER TEN

COOPER strode up Brunswick Street in desperate need of a caffeine fix, entering the first café he came to which happened to bear the interesting name The Red Tongue.

Was there anything about this suburb that wasn't way-out or different or designed to throw him into a spin?

From the minute he'd first set foot here he'd been slightly off-kilter and out of his depth, both foreign feelings that didn't sit well with him. He liked control, order, planning, and forward thinking. Instead, since he'd set his sights on acquiring the gallery nothing had gone according to plan, particularly the conscience he'd suddenly grown.

The same conscience that now screamed he'd let Ariel down somehow, that he'd driven an irreversible wedge between them.

It hadn't been intentional. The proposal was business and he'd hoped that once the deal was behind them she might be interested in catching up on a social level again.

Fat chance.

He could handle her teasing, her loaded barbs, and her occasional put down—but tears?

No way.

The sound of her choked-up voice and the glistening moisture on her cheeks had kicked him in the gut and sent him straight out of there, torn between wanting to comfort her and strangle her for making this deal more complicated than it had to be.

'What'll it be, mate?'

Cooper tried not to stare at the young guy taking his order, but it was pretty hard not to. The kid sported enough metal studded through his face to construct a bridge and had a white G-stripe through his gothic black hair.

'Strong espresso, please.'

'No worries. Coming right up.'

He watched the skunk guy saunter away, slashes in his denim jeans, a less-than-white cloth hanging out of his back pocket and a black T-shirt featuring the café's logo, feeling way older than his thirty years.

He'd never considered himself overly conservative but spending time in this suburb made him feel more ancient than Noah.

Though this place wasn't too bad in the displacement stakes: brown vinyl booths, chrome modern chairs, plain wooden tables. The only eye-catching things in the café were the fire-engine-red menus, those and the metal-favouring staff.

'Here you go.'

Skunk guy returned in record time and placed a steaming espresso in front of Cooper. He wanted to inhaled it, needing a jolt of caffeine to hotwire his brain into coming up with a solution to the Ariel problem.

'Thanks,' Cooper said, stirring two sugars into his

coffee for added oomph and wondering why the waiter hadn't moved. 'Is there something else?'

Skunk guy looked nervous about something, the metal rod in his nose twitching. 'Actually, there is. You look like a guy who'd appreciate art. Here, take a look at this.'

He pulled a flyer from his back pocket—the opposite pocket to the one containing the dirty rag, thank goodness—and slapped it on the table. 'This artist is awesome! She's having her first showing tomorrow and you should go. Tell all your friends.'

Cooper glanced at the flyer as he took his first, welcome sip of coffee, almost snorting it out when he saw where the exhibition would be held.

'Colour by Dreams, featuring Chelsea Lynch.'

The artist's name rang a bell too but he couldn't quite place it immediately.

'It'd be cool if you brought a whole heap of people. The artist really needs support.'

'And who are you? Her PR manager?'

Cooper admired the young guy's push, wondering if he was a friend of Ariel's rather than the artist. It wouldn't surprise him in the least if she had a whole string of guys like this ready to promote and support her.

Look how she had him feeling.

Skunk guy grinned sheepishly. 'No, I'm her boyfriend. Chelsea is the best and I said I'd help her out by passing out some flyers to customers. Hope you don't mind?'

'After you brought me a coffee like this? No problems.'

'You're cool for a business dude,' skunk guy said, giving him some weird hand sign involving his index and little fingers pointing up with the rest of his fingers aiming down before slouching away to try his sales pitch on the next customer.

Cooper picked up the flyer and studied the short bio of Chelsea Lynch: local girl who had grown up in Fitzroy, won scholarship to study art, first showing sponsored by Colour by Dreams.

The last fact interested Cooper more than the rest. Why would Ariel sponsor another artist? Weren't gallery showings as rare as the last piece of prime developing land in this street?

From what he'd read, it took most artists years of hard slog and self-promotion to obtain a showing, yet here was a young artist starting out being sponsored by a gallery?

Cooper drained the rest of his coffee, folded the flyer and tucked it into his jacket pocket, hoping the old adage 'out of sight, out of mind' might work. For some inexplicable reason, he suddenly felt like a big, bad bully for pushing the gallery deal and, in the process, ruining the dreams of people like this new artist.

Not to mention ruining the dreams of another artist.

He had his own agendas, his own goals, but what if Ariel's dreams were just as important as his?

This is business…this is business…

The hard thing was, no matter how many times he told himself it was only business, seeing Ariel's vulnerability had delivered a kick in the guts to his cool, aloof act he'd donned for the presentation.

She'd found a chink in his impenetrable armour and he didn't like it.

Business was one thing, caring about the opposition another and, unfortunately, he'd actually grown to like the fiery artist with the zany dress sense.

Enough to forfeit your dream?

Shaking his head and wishing for a clear-cut solution to this new problematic development in his quest for success, he left payment for the coffee along with a hefty tip and headed for the door.

He didn't make it.

The fiery artist burst through the door and made a beeline straight for him, and by the murderous expression on her face it looked like her tears were a thing of the past and she'd rather skewer someone's head.

His.

'Tell me more about this lease business.'

Ariel resisted the urge to stab Cooper in the chest and settled for plopping into the booth opposite the chair he'd just vacated.

She preferred the soft, comfy vinyl to the hard-backed chairs. Not that his choice surprised her: hard chair for a hard ass.

'Drink?' he offered, sliding back into the chair with obvious reluctance. 'And how did you find me? Is stalking another of your hidden talents?'

Ariel toyed with the cutlery in front of her, particularly the knife, and contemplated all sorts of delightful ways she could use it on the infuriating man opposite her.

'Everyone in the street knows me and when I asked about a tall, uptight guy in a fancy suit the old man from the Nepalese shop pointed me straight here.' She smirked, seeing his frown at her uptight dig. 'And no, thanks, I don't want a drink, I want answers.'

To give him credit, Cooper's sombre expression didn't change. Most guys would've bawled her out for her outrageous behaviour, from sniffling tears to arrogant demands in less than ten minutes. He took it in his stride, leaning back in his chair and folding his arms, his blue-eyed gaze unwavering.

'All the answers are in the proposal you asked me to leave you.'

'I'd rather hear about it from you. Besides, I don't have time to read a whole lot of legalese that you've probably peppered through that doorstopper of a document you prepared.'

Okay, so she sounded ruder by the minute but she couldn't help it. When she was nervous, she got defensive and obnoxious and pushy.

So, he could sue her. Wouldn't be much different from what he was trying to do to her at the moment anyway, ripping out her home and livelihood from under her.

'You could've heard more if you hadn't booted me out of the gallery.'

A challenging gleam glittered in the intelligent blue depths focussed on her and a tiny thrill went through her that here was a guy she could match wits with, who could give as good as he got.

She tilted her chin up and glared him down. 'Could've, should've, would've but didn't. How about you tell me everything you know about that lease now?'

So she could high-tail it straight to the council offices and see if she had an easel to stand on.

He folded his arms, a cool, casual gesture of a confident guy rather than a defence mechanism, and met her stare straight on. 'The council has had a ninety-nine-year lease on the land twice. The original owners, when the land was pastoral, leased it to the council who later bought the lease once the owners offered it to them for a hefty price. As I told you before, your Barb signed a twenty-five year lease with the council, which was extremely generous, and that's up for renewal. However, I've spoken to several people within the council who are ready to negotiate a sale for the right price. If that happens, you get nothing, which is why it's in your best interests to vacate now, take what's on offer and lease elsewhere. That about cover it?'

Ariel listened to every damning word, her heart sinking lower than Cooper's lousy offer.

Could he be right about the council selling or was he toying with her as he had from the start?

Only one way to find out and that was push him.

'The council won't sell. You're bluffing.'

He leaned forwards, placing his forearms on the table and drawing her attention to his long fingers which she'd noticed when painting him. Long fingers that she'd fantasised about, skimming her body, bringing her pleasure…

'I'm telling you how it is.'

She grabbed for a curl and wound it around her finger, meeting his unflinching stare while her insides quaked. He had to be wrong. She couldn't contemplate any other option.

She'd made a promise to Barb, she had a legend to keep up, to continue the work Barb had started in the local community. She'd be a monkey's aunt if she let a guy like Cooper railroad her into making a decision out of fear.

'You've seen enough of this street to know the type of image the council wants to portray and the gallery is a vital part of the local colour. Besides, we do a lot for local talent, not to mention the street kids in the area.'

'Street kids? What's your involvement with them?'

If his upper-class lip had curled in derision, she wouldn't have been surprised. His incredulous tone said it all.

Heat surged into her cheeks, a potent combination of anger and resentment that a guy like him wouldn't understand the first thing about what it was like to be starving, cold and desperate, and that he'd dare question her about it.

'Never mind—it's not relevant to your *business proposal*, is it?'

By the sharp flare of awareness in his eyes, he registered her venom-loaded barb.

Shaking his head, he pushed back from the table. 'Look, this is getting us nowhere. I've answered your question about the lease, I've tried to lay out the offer as plainly as I can. The figures are in the document so once you have a chance to think it over, I'm sure you'll make the right decision. I'll call by later for your decision.'

'Don't bother!'

She leaped to her feet as he stood up, knowing she should shut up and get out before she said something she'd regret but her defensive hackles were well and truly bristling and her thoughts became words faster than she could stop them.

'I'm not interested in anything you have to offer, now or ever. I know you've been hanging around me, acting nice to soften me up, but it hasn't worked. So you storm into the gallery today doing your intimidation act. Which, I hate to tell you, hasn't been successful either. So why don't you quit while you're behind and leave me alone?'

To her amazement, he laughed. 'Does this mean you won't have dinner with me tonight so I can get your final answer?'

She clenched her hands.

'It means I don't want to ever see you again.'

She turned on her heel, hoping her worn flip-flops wouldn't send her sprawling and spoil her attempt at a dignified exit.

'That's going to be hard, considering I've been invited to Chelsea Lynch's showing tomorrow and I'm all for supporting new talent.'

She stiffened as he brushed past her, waving a flyer in her face with a smug smile of his own as he held open the door.

She didn't respond.

She couldn't; it took all her concentration to walk past the guy who, while he couldn't take no for an answer and it annoyed her beyond all reason, stood up to her as no one ever had.

And a huge part of her admired him for it.

She liked this guy.

Against her better judgement, with every instinct screaming they were worlds apart and he spelled trouble with a capital T, she liked him.

Now what was she going to do about it, considering she didn't want to see his smug face ever again?

'Ariel, wait.'

If she'd had half a brain, she would've ignored him and kept going. Instead, there was something in his tone of voice, a softening, which made her halt in her tracks.

'What?'

He broached the short distance between them and took hold of her upper arms; she couldn't have bolted if she'd tried.

'Why did you follow me?'

'Because I'm insane,' she muttered, wriggling in his grip to get free.

It wasn't so much his probing question that had her wanting to flee as much as his touch, his firm hands scorching her with his particular brand of heat. The type of heat that made her lose her mind. Having her arms tingling wasn't enough. She wanted that heat to spread through her body, to have his hands all over her, exploring, caressing, stroking. Every last inch...

'You listened to me in there where you wouldn't back at the gallery. What changed your mind?'

Darn him for being so observant, so persistent.

She stopped wriggling, fixing him with a glare that would've sent a lesser man heading for the hills.

'Fine, you want to hear the truth? I always keep a promise. Simple as that. I felt bad for reneging on my part of the deal when you'd been pretty good about the whole posing thing, so that's it. You happy?'

'I am now,' he murmured, his hands sliding around her waist, moulding her to him, sending her pulse into overdrive and her belly into freefall. 'I'm not the enemy, you know.'

'Says who?'

She tried to pull back but his arms tightened, pinning her against him. Logic told her to make a run for it, but desire flowed through her body and made her wish he'd drag her back to the gallery this second and make love to her. Maybe once they got rid of all this pent-up tension, she might be able to steel herself against him once and for all?

Or maybe she was making excuses for wanting to get naked with the hottest guy she'd ever known?

'I can prove it to you,' he said, tilting her chin up to gaze into her eyes, his blue eyes boring into her with an intense expression she couldn't fathom.

'Prove what?'

She'd lost track of the conversation the second her mind had put the two of them together naked.

'Prove I'm not the enemy.'

'And how are you going to do that? By schmoozing me?'

'Don't tempt me.' His gaze dropped to her lips and her breath hitched.

Kiss me, you fool!

Her lips parted and for an insane second, she wondered if she'd spoken aloud.

His head descended, blocking out the brilliant sunshine streaming down on them, and she held her breath, her hands splayed on his chest, craving the feel of bare skin rather than expensive cotton.

Her eyelids fluttered shut and she tilted her head a fraction, craving the touch of his lips more than she'd craved anything in her entire life.

'I'll call you,' he said against the corner of her mouth, his lips brushing hers in the briefest of almost-there kisses before pulling away.

What the—?

Her eyes snapped open and she reeled from the disappointment of another missed kiss from the most infuriating guy she'd ever met.

He stepped away and she steadied her legs, knowing if she swayed towards him he'd know how truly pathetic she really was. One minute she was telling him to get lost, the next she was offering herself up like some virgin sacrifice to the Vikings.

'Whatever,' she said, brushing an errant curl out of her face, turning the gesture into a casual wave as he smiled, gave her a smart salute and walked away.

However, there was nothing remotely casual about the blood pounding through her body or how much she wanted the guy who had the potential to ruin her once and for all.

CHAPTER ELEVEN

'WHY the glum face, *bella*?'

Ariel summoned a smile for Sofia, knowing it fell well short of her usual beam when the Italian woman's dark eyes filled with concern.

'My muse is being stubborn,' Ariel said, fiddling with the dimmer switch on the gallery lights, wanting to get the ambience just right before opening the doors to the public in ten minutes for Chelsea's show.

Sofia tapped her upper lip with a manicured, crimson fingernail. 'Are you sure it's just your muse being stubborn?'

'What do you mean?'

Ariel stepped back and studied the vibrant oil landscape in front of her, pleased with the vivid colours dancing beneath a soft spotlight.

'Maybe that delicious man has you in a spin and you're holding out on him? *Santo cielo*, what a dish that one is!'

Sofia kissed her fingertips and waved them heavenward—holy sky indeed!—while Ariel smiled, a genuine, from-the-heart smile, her first since her confrontation with Mr Big-Shot yesterday.

'That kind of dish gives me indigestion so I'd rather not talk about him.'

She should've known not to deny anything too vehemently with Sofia. It only served to inflame her curiosity.

'A-h-h-h...a lover's quarrel, perhaps?' Sofia's eyes sparkled with intrigue. 'All great love affairs need drama and I think you have this with your young man, no?'

'No! And he's not my young man.'

Ariel moved onto her next task, making sure the cheese platters were arranged just right and interspersed with the exotic dips and crackers, wondering why a small, traitorous part of her soul wished he were.

'*Bella*, life does not have to be so tough all the time. What will be will be.'

Concern laced Sofia's words while Ariel mentally disagreed.

Life was tough. At least, hers always had been and she didn't know any better. Losing the gallery would be just another example of it. A sad, heart-breaking example as she lost the one thing that symbolised hope to her: hope for a better life, hope that good things could come out of bad, hope that she could be the type of person Barb would've wanted her to be.

The type of person she wanted to be: successful, proud and independent. Qualities guys like Cooper took for granted.

Well, she'd show him.

If she could rustle up a cool million or so, that was.

'If there is anything I can do to help...' Sofia trailed off, quirking a stencilled eyebrow while draping a plump arm across her shoulders.

'I'll be fine,' Ariel said, submitting to a quick hug

before shrugging out of Sofia's embrace, wondering if the lie sounded as hollow to Sofia as it did to her.

She wouldn't be fine, considering the council had confirmed her greatest fear this morning: they were selling the land the gallery stood on.

Like most councils around Melbourne, they were strapped for cash and in desperate need of more schools and health-care facilities. So selling off the last piece of prime real estate in Brunswick Street was a no-brainer.

Of course, they'd given her an option. Come up with the cash herself or lose the gallery.

Some option.

For a person struggling to meet the monthly rent, they might as well have handed her a rope knotted into a noose.

'Hey, you guys. Do you think everything looks okay?' Chelsea bounded up to them, red hair gelled into fearsome spikes, a funky beige leather ensemble draping her lithe body.

Ariel pasted a smile on her face and sent Sofia a pointed look to change the subject. 'Relax. Your paintings look great and this showing is going to be a hit.'

Chelsea's confident grin waned. 'What if no one comes?'

'Pah! Do not worry, *bambina*. I have told the whole of Melbourne. Everyone will be here!' Sofia flung her arms wide and Chelsea straightened, her confidence restored.

Ariel sent Sofia a grateful glance, wishing her problems could be solved as easily. 'Chelsea, why don't you make sure the inventory list and red sale dots are in order while Sofia checks on the wine?'

While she scooted out the back to brace herself for Cooper's appearance.

Surely he wouldn't show?

He'd probably been trying to intimidate her again by saying he'd come to Chelsea's showing, wanting to up the pressure, turn the screws a little tighter.

Well, she had news for him.

If he did show his sorry face here tonight, she'd be the only one doing any screwing over.

She'd thought long and hard about her options all afternoon while preparing the gallery, and as much as Cooper's offer seemed her only chance at getting a fresh start elsewhere, she couldn't do it.

Taking his money would be selling out on her dream, selling out on her promise to Barb, and she wouldn't let that happen. She couldn't.

She would fight this with every weapon in her limited arsenal. Approaching the National Trust, the Arts Council, the Victorian Grants Committee. Whatever it took, she would do it.

People depended on her, people like Chelsea who would never have a chance at discovery if it weren't for the gallery and Barb's legacy. As she watched the young red-haired woman flit around the gallery one last time to ensure everything was in order she knew there was no other choice.

She could never sell out and if Cooper or the local council wanted this piece of land, they would have to drag her screaming from it after she'd exhausted every avenue.

'Ariel, there's a crowd outside. Shall I open the door?' Chelsea's hushed tone alerted Ariel to just how nervous the young woman was, for Chelsea never spoke in anything below a dull roar.

'Go ahead. It's your moment to shine,' Ariel said, giving Chelsea's arm a reassuring squeeze, fervently hoping this wouldn't be the girl's first and last showing at Colour by Dreams.

He came.

Ariel knew the exact moment Cooper set foot in the gallery because the hair on her nape stood to attention. So did most of the women in the room.

To give her credit, she averted her gaze after the first soul-wrenching moment when their eyes met and what could only be described as sizzling heat arced between them.

But that one, loaded moment was all it took for her to imprint his powerful image on her brain: black jeans, black T-shirt, black leather jacket, the bad-boy wardrobe looking way too good on uptight Mr Big-Shot.

Throw in the sardonic glint in his too-blue eyes and a natural confidence that turned heads and she knew she'd have trouble getting through the rest of the evening.

He could've played fair and avoided her.

Of course, he didn't.

'You can run but you can't hide,' Cooper said, sneaking up on her in the studio kitchenette while she hunted for extra plastic cups under the sink.

Ariel's head snapped up and she avoided clunking it on the rusty metal sink by a millimetre.

'Nice view, by the way.'

With heat flushing her cheeks, she wriggled backwards from her awkward position and hoped her butt didn't look big in the crushed velvet hot-pants before mentally slapping herself for caring.

'What are you doing here? I told you not to come.'

He leaned against the door jamb and raised an eyebrow, sending her pulse hammering. 'In answer to your first question, I'm here because I'm interested in art. As for you telling me not to come, surely you know that I love a challenge?'

She clenched the bag of cheap plastic cups in her hand till they crackled. 'That's what I am to you, isn't it? A challenge. "Let's see how much I can suck up to the flighty artist and watch her capitulate and hand me her gallery on a platter." Well, I've got news for you, boyo. It ain't going to happen!'

She expected him to frown, to glower, to get that stern business look on his face he'd had yesterday when he'd presented his lousy pitch.

Instead, his infuriating smile widened.

'You're stunning when you're angry.'

A tiny thrill of happiness shot through her—a girl had her pride, after all—before she fixed him with a glare designed to intimidate. 'And you're full of it. Now, if you don't mind, I have to get back out there.'

'Oh, but I do mind,' he murmured as she attempted to push past him and, short of plastering her body against his in the doorway, she stopped dead and waited for him to lower his arm.

He did.

Only as far as her waist.

'You can keep running from me all night but I'm not going anywhere. We need to talk and I'm not leaving till that happens.'

He spoke softly, his words dripping with gentle persuasion, but she barely registered them as the light touch of his hand resting on her waist sent her into a tailspin.

The warmth from his palm scorched through the snug velvet hugging her waist, branding her skin and enticing her to do all sorts of crazy things such as slide into his arms and get an all-over body experience of that seductive warmth.

She knew his touch didn't mean a thing.

She knew flirting was second nature to a successful guy like him.

And she knew without a shadow of a doubt that she should boot him out the door so quickly he wouldn't have time to register it.

Instead, she tilted her chin up, looked him straight in the eye and said, 'If you're sticking around, make yourself useful. I could do with a spare pair of hands.'

With that, she picked his hand off her waist, holding it a fraction too long before dropping it and walking away without a backward glance.

'What a night.'

Ariel flopped onto a sofa, slid her three-inch cork wedges off and rubbed her aching feet, wishing a cup of tea would miraculously appear before her.

'Would you like something to drink? A nice hot cup of tea perhaps?'

Cooper squatted down in front of her, still looking bright-eyed and bushy-tailed while she felt like a washed-out rag. Darn him.

'I knew I let you stay for a reason,' she said, hating the way her heart lurched at the sweet expression on his face, at the way his lips curved up in a smile and at the way he read her mind and knew exactly what she needed at that precise moment. 'A cup of blackcurrant and apple tea would be great.'

He grimaced. 'That combo belongs in kiddies' fruit drinks.'

'It's delicious. Then again, a caffeine addict like you wouldn't have a clue.'

She softened her dig with a smile and his answering grin warmed her from the inside out and better than any cup of tea ever had.

'You sit tight and this clueless coffee connoisseur will bring you your poison in a jiffy.'

Ariel watched him straighten and stride away, admiring the way the black denim moulded his butt and his long, lean legs.

She shouldn't have let him stay.

She should've booted him out with the rest of the stragglers, mainly an exuberant Chelsea and matchmaking Sofia, but she hadn't had the energy. Besides, there was nothing he could say that would change her mind about selling the gallery and she wanted to make that clear.

Once she outlined her plans for raising the necessary funds, she had no doubt that she'd see the back of Cooper Vance.

She should be rapt.

Instead, an empty feeling blossomed in the vicinity of her heart and spread outward, icy tentacles of loneliness creeping through her and making her wish for all sorts of futile things.

She wished Cooper weren't a take-all businessman.

She wished they'd met under different circumstances.

Scariest of all, she wished she didn't have a huge crush on a guy who had no interest in her other than as a means to an end.

'Here we are, one cup of hot fruit punch as requested. Gross.'

Cooper handed her a steaming cup of tea and she inhaled the irresistible fruity aroma, sighing with pleasure after her first sip.

'Thanks. This is heaven,' she said, tucking her feet under her and taking blissful sips while studying Cooper over the rim of her cup.

'You're easily pleased if that's your idea of heaven,' he said, taking a seat next to her on the sofa, his proximity setting off warning bells in her head.

She could've scuttled away like a frightened mouse but lethargy infused her body. She simply didn't have the energy to move, or the inclination, if she were completely honest.

What did she expect to happen anyway? For the guy to kiss her senseless? As if.

You wish.

The stupid thing was, she did and she took several gulps of hot tea to wash away the thought.

'You're not having anything?'

He shook his head. 'I'm fine. Are you?'

Before she could decipher what he meant, he reached across the short space separating them and skimmed his fingertips across her cheek. 'You look worn out.'

'I haven't been sleeping well,' she muttered, glaring at the main cause of her insomnia and wishing he'd revert to uncaring business mode.

She could handle that guy.

This softer, astute version of Cooper had the power to undo her in a second.

'Guess that's partly my fault, huh?'

'There's no partly about it. It's all your fault.'

His eyes widened and for an embarrassing second she wondered if he knew exactly how he affected her.

'Having you breathing down my neck, trying to oust me from this place, hasn't been pleasant,' she rushed on, focussing on the business side of things in the hope he wouldn't delve deeper and realise there was more to her sleepless nights than worrying about the gallery's future. 'It's stressful, and you're talking to a person who doesn't do stress. Yoga, yeah. Meditation, yeah. Stress, uh-uh.'

He pulled away from her, a tiny frown indenting his brow. 'It doesn't have to be stressful if you'd listen to reason.'

Anger shot through her and she placed her near empty cup on the floor. 'Reason being?'

'I'm not going to rehash old ground,' he said, leaning back in his corner of the sofa and spreading his arms across the top, looking way too confident. 'You know that my offer is fair, considering the council can oust you once the lease is up and you'll be left with nothing.'

'How about I throw you out of here right now?'

She leaned closer, refraining from jabbing him in the chest at the last second. 'Or, better yet, you finally get the message that I'm not interested in anything you have to offer, ever, and walk on out of here of your own accord?'

His eyes darkened to midnight-blue as he sat forward and lowered his arms. 'You're lying. I think you're very interested in what I have to offer.'

Her heart thudded at his loaded response, at his

nearness. He smelt so good, an intoxicating blend of sandalwood and something lighter that evoked a powerful response in her. She loved scents: fresh flowers, aromatherapy oils, rain on freshly cut grass, but none of her favourite smells came close to Cooper's heady scent.

Damn the man, he knew how he affected her and he was rubbing her nose in it.

Well, she'd show him.

'You're delusional. And if you're trying to imply there's something behind the weird flirting thing we do occasionally, forget it. We both know you're slumming it for a while, getting to know how the other half live.'

His jaw clenched, his eyes narrowed and tension radiated off him in palpable waves.

She moved in for the kill. If this didn't get him out of her life once and for all, nothing would.

'Don't worry, I'm a big girl, I can take it. You spend time with the eccentric artist, flirt a little, soften her up, get her to buy into your crazy scheme. I get it. It's the way you do business. Take no prisoners, tell no lies and all that. Hey, no hard feelings.'

Though he was right; she was lying.

At least about the feelings part.

She had feelings and plenty of them. The problem was she couldn't do anything about them. Her life was complicated enough without letting her erratic emotions join the party.

'Are you finished?' he said, his tone low, menacing.

'Actually, I haven't. I also think you're snobby, condescending and—'

His lips crushed hers into silence and she gasped in

shock, realising a second too late that opening her mouth might be construed as an invitation.

Cooper didn't hesitate, deepening the kiss, challenging her to meet him halfway, coercing her with a skilful precision that took her breath away.

Well, he wasn't the only one who liked a challenge and in the split second where reason warred with passion she threw caution to the wind and showed him exactly who he was messing with.

Her lips clung to his, frantic, desperate, meshing in a whirlpool of hot sensation that lit a fire deep within.

Her hands took on a life of their own, skimming the wall of his rock-hard chest before sliding higher, tangling in his hair to pull his head closer, to anchor herself in a world tilting crazily out of control.

Heat streaked through her body and she leaned into him, wanting more, needing more, and as his arms slid around her, hauling her across his body to lie on top of him, logic fled only to be replaced by a deep-seated yearning that this should go on for ever.

Cooper broke the kiss to stare into her eyes, his hands pushing the curls off her face in a gentle caress.

She couldn't fathom the expression in his eyes and reality hit as he shifted slightly beneath her. Here she was, lying on top of an extremely hot guy, a guy she could easily fall for in the blink of an eye if she completely lost her mind, a guy she'd been in the process of dismissing from her life a few moments ago, a guy who had just sent her spiralling out of control with a simple kiss.

What on earth was she doing?

Okay, so maybe the kiss hadn't been so simple. In fact, it had been downright amazing. But that wasn't the point. She still needed to get rid of him, and fast. No telling what her kick-started desire might do in the next ten seconds or so.

Disengaging his hands from her face, she slid onto the floor in an undignified heap before leaping to her feet like some bumbling clown act in a circus. 'Well, that was an interesting diversion but I hate to tell you, it didn't work. I still want you to get out of here.'

Cooper stood with a lot more grace than she had, his inscrutable expression annoying her. Couldn't the guy at least look the teensiest bit shaken by the cataclysmic kiss they'd shared? Then again, maybe it wasn't so extraordinary for him. He probably went around kissing half the female population in Melbourne like that.

And, no, that sharp stab of pain in the vicinity of her heart wasn't jealousy; it had to be all that cheese she'd consumed earlier mixing with the tea to give her heartburn.

'If you don't shut up, I'm going to kiss you again till you do.'

She opened her mouth with an instant rebuke, but shut it quickly as he took a threatening step towards her.

Then again, the thought of more of that sensational kissing wasn't so bad...

'Good, now that I've got your attention, I want you to listen up. Yes, I want this deal to go through and, yes, it's very important to me. In fact, it's more than important, it's imperative.'

He paused for a moment as if searching for the right words and she waited, prepared to give him a little leeway. After all, it was the least she could do before she booted him out the door permanently.

'As for what's happening between you and me, it's

got nothing to do with business. Do I wish you were some shriveled-up old prune that wouldn't tempt me? Yeah. Do I wish I could completely separate business from everything about you that entices me? Yeah. Do I wish I could seal this deal and not look back without remembering the curve of your smile, the fire in your eyes, the passion of your kiss? You bet. But there's no use wishing for the impossible and, right now, pretending that something doesn't exist between us would be doing just that and I won't. I can't.'

Ariel's jaw hit the floor and her mind whirled as Cooper stared her down, the bad-boy businessman daring her to disagree.

Okay, so he was man enough to acknowledge the spark between them. Big deal.

That didn't mean she had to agree with him or encourage him, despite how her heart raced at the wonderful things he'd said about her and the fact he found her just as attractive as she found him.

He was still the enemy and would still tear her world apart given half a chance.

A chance she had no intention of giving him.

'Got nothing to say? Come on, give it your best shot,' he said, the grim look in his eyes at odds with the sardonic half-smile playing about his lips.

'What do you want me to say?'

Apart from the obvious: I like you, I desire you, I can easily lose my head and go crazy for you.

But then, she wasn't the type of girl to lose her head. She had too much at stake, too many responsibilities, starting with making the gallery a viable proposition for the next umpteen years just as Barb would've wanted.

'How about you start with the truth?'

Ariel compressed her lips, a simple, defensive gesture to prevent her from blurting a whole host of truths that Cooper wouldn't want to hear: the truth was, she was petrified the gallery would slip through her fingers despite how hard she'd worked to keep it afloat, she was petrified she'd let everyone down and, the biggie of them all, she was petrified of how this guy made her feel.

So, despite her usual trait for brutal honesty, she opted for the easy way out.

She lied.

'There isn't anything between us beyond the usual guy-girl chemistry. We're opposites in every way and you want something from me I can't give you, *imperative* or not.'

Avoiding his penetrating stare, she continued, 'I won't sell, you don't get what you want and we have no reason to keep meeting like this so let's call it quits while we're both still being civil to one another, okay?'

She expected him to bamboozle her with a whole lot of convoluted arguments, similar to the ones in his long-winded business proposal, to change her mind.

She expected him to pressure her, to ram home the reasons why obtaining *her* gallery was so darn *imperative* to him.

Instead, he surprised her yet again.

He took a step forward, invading her personal space with his overpowering presence, and she resisted the urge to lean into him, to experience the thrill of having his arms slide around her one last time and making her forget every single reason why they couldn't be together.

Placing a finger under her chin, he gently tipped it

up and stared into her eyes. 'You know the interesting thing about chemistry? It can lead to explosive reactions and unexpected outcomes.'

She should look away.

She wanted to look away.

Instead, she stared at him like a hypnotised dummy while his thumb brushed her bottom lip with infinite tenderness and he smiled, a hot, loaded smile.

'Oh, and one more thing. Chemistry was my best subject.'

Before she could gather her wits and tell him exactly what he could do with his subjects, he pulled her into his arms and kissed her.

This was her last chance.

Push him away, and ignore all the great things he'd said about her.

He deepened the kiss, his hands winding through her curls, angling her head for better access, and the second his tongue touched hers she lost it.

The point of no return.

She pushed him back against the sofa, her hands everywhere, sliding under black cotton, stroking the hot skin of his tight abs beneath.

Someone moaned, a low, sexy sound, and in the passionate haze that had invaded her brain she had no idea if it was him or her. Nor did she care.

The scent of him, the feel of him, the taste of him, the sounds of ragged breathing and low moans set a spark to her latent libido.

'You sure about this?'

Cooper broke the kiss for a second, capturing her face in his hands, staring deep into her eyes.

'Shut up and kiss me,' she said, the blatant lust radiating from his too-blue gaze setting fire to any tiny residual doubt she might have harboured and sending it up in smoke.

'Your call.'

And he did exactly as she'd instructed, with one heck of a difference.

He didn't hold back.

Their mouths clashed in a heated frenzy of lips and tongues, challenging, duelling, an erotic game where there were no losers, only winners.

Ariel sighed as his lips slid down her throat and she arched against him, bringing her into direct contact with his erection, his very impressive erection if the size of his hardness against her belly was any indication.

'God, you're beautiful,' he said, his lips ceasing their leisurely exploration as he swiftly unbuttoned her top and peeled it open, the anticipatory gleam in his eyes like that of a man opening the best present ever.

The few times she'd had sex in the past, she'd hated the undressing bit. Inadequacies had plagued her growing up, and they manifested at the oddest of times, such as now when she hoped her boobs weren't a disappointment and he wouldn't find her too skinny.

'Stunning,' he breathed, unclipping her bra with a deft flick of his fingers and staring at her breasts as if he'd found treasure, before capturing a nipple in his mouth.

'That feels so good,' she murmured, writhing beneath him, wishing their clothes would disappear, burning up from the inside.

'You feel so good.'

And he set about proving it, drawing his tongue

slowly across her chest, sucking one nipple then the other, feasting on her as if he hadn't eaten in a decade.

Ariel throbbed in so many places she didn't know whether she should shock the living daylights out of Cooper and devour him now or prolong the sweet agony and let him continue to lavish her with more of the exquisite licking and sucking that was sending her into meltdown.

'I need you,' she whispered, proving just how much by sliding a hand between them and cupping his erection.

Cooper tensed, muttered a very sexy curse and pulled away, staring at her in such a searing way that desire shot through her veins, her nipples pebbled and a heaviness settled in her core.

'Now.'

He hovered over her, a sexy smile playing around his mouth. 'You know you're bossy and sassy and thoroughly irresistible, don't you?'

'I'll show you bossy.'

She surged upwards, her hands against his chest, pushing him upright against the back of the sofa and straddling him.

He laughed, a low, rich, wicked sound that provoked her to show him just how bossy she could be.

She whipped his T-shirt over his head in a second, leaning forward to nuzzle his neck and drape her hair across his bare chest. He groaned and she smiled, a small, self-satisfied smile of a woman who knew she had the power to drive a guy crazy.

'Hmm…think you're in charge, huh?'

His hands spanned her waist, holding her in place while he shifted beneath her, leaving her in little doubt that the second their clothes vanished down below, she'd be in heaven.

'You ain't seen nothing yet,' she said, sliding off him to kneel at his feet, her fingers making short work of his zipper and button, easing the denim down his long legs with her gaze locked on his the entire time.

His low moan turned her on.

His glazed look empowered her.

His stirring erection beneath tight black boxers encouraged her to toy with the elastic, brush her fingertips against his penis and slowly, tantalisingly peel the cotton down his legs.

'Oh, wow,' she said, sitting on her heels and admiring the view. A very hard, very large erection was standing to attention, liquid heat pooling between her legs as she reached out to stroke it.

'Hell, Ariel,' Cooper gritted out, hanging onto what little self-control he had left when her hand wrapped around his shaft and started moving up and down in slow, rhythmic movements.

'Don't you mean heaven?'

Her sassy mouth curved into a knowing smile as she flicked her thumb over the hood, sending him into overdrive.

'You're a minx.'

He stilled her hand, sliding to the floor next to her, grateful for the soft, plush rug over the boards.

'Hey, what happened to me being in charge?'

'My turn,' he said, knowing he couldn't last much longer.

He'd been fantasising about Ariel for too long, wondering what she'd look like naked, wondering what colour her nipples would be, wondering how she'd sound when he took her.

Her breasts were gorgeous, a perfect handful, with dusky pink nipples that stood out at the slightest provocation. Considering his hands and mouth hadn't left them alone since he'd taken off her top, they were very provoked.

Now, he had to see the rest of her, taste the rest of her, feel her hot and tight around him before he lost it completely.

Sliding a slow, sensual kiss across her swollen lips, he had those sexy little hot-pants off her in one smooth tug. The red satin G-string beneath got tangled up at the same time and when he broke the kiss to stare down at her, his sigh bordered on reverence.

'You're stunning. Every exquisite inch.'

He kissed her again, softly this time, teasing, pleasing as his fingers delved in her moist heat, finding her nub and circling it with his thumb, loving the small, excited sounds she made in his mouth.

She broke off the kiss, her head falling back, her breathing ragged as he slid two fingers inside her, his thumb stroking her folds, her clitoris, with increasing pressure.

'Cooper.'

Their gazes locked as she convulsed around his fingers, her body arching upwards, her orgasm heating the gold flecks in her eyes till they glowed amber.

He had to have her, right at that precise second, with her soft and pliant and sated in his arms.

'More.'

He stared at her sassy mouth, knowing a woman like

Ariel would be a never-ending source of surprises and hoping he'd get an opportunity to discover them all.

Though he wasn't a fool.

This was sex and she'd probably withdraw from him in a big way in the morning. Not if he had his way. This attraction had been simmering between them right from the very beginning and he had no intention of letting this be a one-night stand.

Besides, he had a feeling sex with the stunning artist could become addictive. Very addictive. And he didn't have too many vices.

'More, huh? Boy, there's no pleasing some women.'

'I'm pleased all right,' she said. 'You, on the other hand, could do with a bit of pleasuring yourself.'

She sent a pointed look at his groin, her fingers closing around his erection, and he groaned.

'Hold that...thought,' he said, fumbling through the back pocket of his jeans for his wallet, grabbing a condom and ripping open the little blue foil packet while Ariel continued to stroke him, her sexy laugh driving him as insane as her hand.

Ariel loved the silky hardness of Cooper's penis, loved the fact she turned him on. She reluctantly released him, watching him slide the condom on, her insides constricting at the thought that she'd soon be sheathing him just as effectively.

'Hurry,' she said, wondering when she'd become such a floozy and not particularly caring.

She wanted Cooper.

Inside her, pleasuring her, hard and hot and pounding, satisfying the ache that had begun the first time he'd taken off his clothes for her.

'Come here.'

Cooper opened his arms to her and Ariel didn't hesitate, straddling him, kissing him, revelling in the tip of his penis nudging at her entrance as she sank down, almost passing out with sheer satisfaction as he stretched her, filled her.

'You feel…' he groaned, loudly, as she raised up and sank down again, taking him in deeper, relaxing her muscles around him, savouring the fullness, the heat.

'Good?'

'Sensational.'

She lost it after that. Thankfully, he did too. Her hands tangled in his hair, she bit into his shoulder as he thrust upwards so hard she almost hit the ceiling and he flipped her over, driving into her with a wild pounding that sent them both into orbit.

Her abandoned scream matched his noisy groan and as she floated back to her senses her first thought was, That was absolutely incredible.

Closely followed by, What the heck have I done?

CHAPTER TWELVE

PALE gold filtered through the tiny bathroom window, heralding the dawn of another perfect Melbourne day.

Though it wasn't just another day.

Ariel braced herself on the antique washbasin, staring at her tousled reflection in the bevelled mirror.

You had sex with Cooper Vance.

And not just ordinary sex. Scintillating, mind-blowing, burn-up-the-sheets sex, though they'd never quite made it to the bed till later. Much later.

She'd never be able to look at her favourite rug in the studio again without remembering the way he'd felt inside her, the way he'd touched her all over, the way he'd made her crave him with every turned-on cell in her body.

The man was a menace.

She'd known it from the first second he'd set foot in her studio and now she had proof. And how!

Closing her eyes, she leaned forward and rested her forehead against the cool glass. What had she done?

She'd been doing her level best to push him away, to ignore the sizzling attraction between them, to focus on saving her business—which meant getting as far from corporate Mr Big-Shot as possible.

Instead, she'd melted into a puddle of lust the minute he'd kissed her and nothing would ever be the same again.

At least, not for her.

She didn't do casual sex, never had. She could count her past encounters on one hand and each had been with guys she'd been dating for a while, boyfriends. The scary thing was, nothing about last night with Cooper felt casual. She felt as if she knew him and that was what scared her more than the way she'd been with him. Or how much she'd enjoyed it.

'You okay?'

Ariel jerked upright and her eyes flew open; she wished she'd kept them tightly shut. The sight of Cooper, a very naked Cooper, reflected all too clearly in the mirror and her heart flipped.

'Fine. Just a bit tired.'

'I'm not surprised.'

He smiled, a warm, intimate smile that notched up the temperature in the bathroom by a hundred degrees.

'I didn't mean to wake you,' she said, fiddling with the tie of her favourite kimono, wishing he'd stop staring at her as if he were starving and she were breakfast. 'I'm usually up pretty early.'

'No problems.'

Silence stretched between them, an awkward, tense silence she would've given anything to avoid. Why couldn't he get dressed and get the heck out of her life? Why couldn't he stop gawking at her?

'You're okay about what happened last night, right?'

To her annoyance, she blushed. 'Fine.'

'You sure about that?'

She stiffened as he came up behind her and slid his arms around her waist, leaving her no option but to lean back against him or jump up on the antique vanity.

'You're gorgeous,' he murmured, nuzzling her neck, sending shivers through her body, resurrecting erotic memories of the way he'd kissed every inch of her last night. Every inch…

'And you're crazy,' she said, taking in her blonde frizzy hair, her swollen lips, which looked as if they'd been ravaged all night—pretty darn close to it!—and her eyes, large and luminous and filled with fear.

Fear of where to now, fear of how much she'd miss him once he exited her life, fear of never finding a guy to make her feel half as good as he'd made her feel last night.

'Whose fault is that?' He kissed his way up her neck, turning her around slowly, staring deep into her eyes. 'You make me crazy. With your sexy smile, with your incredible eyes, with that mouth that makes me want to do everything I did with you last night and so much more.'

'You can cut the sweet talk. I'm a sure thing, remember?'

'Time for you to shut that sassy mouth of yours. Again,' he said, lowering his lips to hers in a slow, sensual kiss that would've curled her toes if she hadn't been standing on them to reach up, desperate for his kiss, hating her treacherous body for it.

'I thought you said you didn't have any more condoms?'

By the feel of his erection pressing against her stomach, she guessed he wasn't popping into the bathroom for a quick goodbye. More like a quickie something else.

'I don't.' His hands strummed her back through the silk of her kimono, the slow, steady rhythm making her arch like a cat. Next she'd be purring. 'Don't worry, we won't need them. I was only planning on taking a shower, that's it.'

But that wasn't it.

He tugged on the knotted tie and slid his hands under the front of her kimono, skimming her skin, teasing with his touch, brushing her nipples with his thumbs till they peaked in sweet agony.

Her breath hitched as he slid the silk from her body with infinite patience, one exquisite inch at a time till the kimono pooled at their feet in a slash of vibrant emerald-green against the white tiles.

'I don't think my shower's big enough for the both of us,' she said, eyeing the small glass cubicle with suspicion, considering Cooper took up most of the bathroom already.

'All the better for a nice close fit.'

With an arm firmly draped around her waist to prevent escape—great, the guy was a mind-reader too?—he turned on the hot and cold taps, tested the water temp and took the opportunity to turn the five-second wait into another scorching kiss.

She could've shrugged out of his grip.

She could've picked up her kimono and stalked from the bathroom with what little dignity she had left intact.

But then, where was the fun in that?

She'd spent a lifetime being serious, first surviving and later being the model niece for Barb. And more recently, worrying her head off about how to keep the gallery afloat. She never had time for fun.

For that was what this last taste of Cooper would be: pure, unadulterated fun.

'You coming in? The water's warm.'

He didn't force her, standing there wearing nothing but a sexy, persuasive smile, his arm loosely draped around her waist.

Now or never...

Sending him a coy glance from beneath her lashes, she said, 'You bet,' and stepped with him into the shower.

A staunch environmentalist, Ariel conserved water by taking minimal showers even though she loved the hot spray peppering her skin. Today, however, her ideals flew out the window along with her reservations as she leaned against Cooper, her back wedged against his front, while his hands travelled her body in long, slow strokes, soaping, circling, teasing, turning her legs to jelly before he delved between them and brought her to a screaming orgasm with a few deft flicks of his fingers.

'You're a dangerous woman,' he said, pulling her into a tight hug that squeezed the breath out of her. Or was it the intensity in his blue-eyed stare that robbed her of the normal function of air-in, air-out?

'Not really. But I can be.'

She sent him a smile designed to entice, a smile filled with promise.

He'd given her so much pleasure, it was time to return the favour. In spades.

Reaching between them, she captured his erection in her hand, stroking it till he groaned, loving the ecstasy etched on his face as she moved harder, faster, till he came in a hot rush.

His head had fallen back, exposing the strong column

of his neck, and she placed a gentle kiss there, knowing they could never recapture this moment, shocked by how sad that made her feel.

Neither spoke.

Instead, Cooper opened his eyes, smiled and rested his forehead against hers, not moving, not saying a word.

And as the water sprayed down on them Ariel knew why.

They had nothing to say.

After all, what could you say when you'd just slept with the enemy?

Cooper knew the precise time his revamped proposal had been delivered to Ariel: ten o'clock. It was now ten twenty-five and it would've taken her exactly twenty-five minutes to high-tail it to Vance Corporation in the Central Business District of Melbourne, including the time she would've spent jumping up and down on the spot having a tantrum.

She wasn't going to like the amendments he'd made to the proposal.

In fact, if the ruckus outside his office door was any indication, she intended on making her feelings known to all and sundry before she even made it into his office.

As he pushed back from his desk and strode across his office the door flung open.

'You've got a nerve!' Ariel shouted, making a beeline for him while Beryl, his secretary, gave an apologetic shrug and made crazy signs with her finger circling her temple.

'I'll take it from here, thanks, Beryl,' he said, walking straight past Ariel to shut the door.

Not that it would make much difference. Half of Flinders Street would've heard Ariel's indignant shriek as she whirled and advanced on him, her eyes filled with emerald fire and her curls bristling about her like a fuzzy halo.

Not that there was anything remotely angelic about the woman considering what they'd got up to last night and in the shower first thing this morning.

'Why don't you take a seat and we discuss the new developments like two rational adults?'

'Rational?'

She drew back her shoulders, drawing his attention to her breasts straining against the Paisley halter top that moulded her like a second skin, eliciting erotic memories of the way she'd felt lying on top of him last night, passionate, feverish, responsive, like a fantasy come to life.

'You expect me to be rational when you have a courier deliver me this?'

Reaching into a huge straw carryall, she flung a sheaf of papers onto his desk and planted her hands on her hips, looking like an avenging Amazon come to slay him. 'Tell me this isn't what it looks like.'

'What does it look like?'

He shouldn't antagonise her further, he really shouldn't, but a small part of him was enjoying their confrontation.

She'd had all the comebacks last night, shooting him down in flames when all he'd tried to do was lay the foundations for a possible future relationship.

She'd hadn't listened to him, she hadn't acknowl-edged his honesty and she sure as hell hadn't given them a chance even after the most mind-blowing sex. Several times.

If he were completely honest with himself, he didn't know if he wanted a future with this woman but he'd be damned if he walked away without exploring the fireworks that exploded whenever they were within two feet of each other.

She was confusing business with pleasure and the only way he knew to bring this to quick closure was to finish the business and move onto more of the pleasure. A lot more...of her soft lips clinging to his, her hands all over his body, her excited little moans as he licked her to orgasm...

'What is wrong with you?' She broached the short distance between them and snapped her fingers in front of his face. 'Cut the vague act and start explaining.'

Wrestling his raging libido into some semblance of control, he headed for the safety of his desk and away from Ariel's intoxicating scent. He'd never smelt anything like it and the weird perfume he could now label as neroli thanks to the tiny essential-oil vial he'd spied in her bag the other day had grown on him. A lot. He doubted he'd ever smell oranges again without remembering the blonde goddess with the eyes of green fire.

'Would you like a drink?'

'No! I would like an explanation. Now.'

She grudgingly plopped into the leather chair opposite his and folded her arms, looking like a recalcitrant schoolgirl waiting for punishment from the principal.

He sat down, straightening the messy papers scattered on his desk, hoping a few extra seconds would help calm her down.

When he caught her eye and saw the narrow green slits glowing with anger, he knew a few extra hours wouldn't help.

'If you've read the amendments, you don't need an explanation. It's pretty clear.'

'The part where you're threatening me or the part where you'll do anything to get your grubby hands on the gallery?'

She leaned forward, her fingers clenching his desk till the knuckles whitened. 'Oops, silly me. The gallery doesn't mean a thing to you, it's the land you're after. I really must learn to clarify my terms, just like you have in this pathetic excuse for a proposal.'

He let her vent. He'd expected the animosity, the antagonism, but it hurt nonetheless.

He cared about her.

And he hadn't realised how much till just now when she looked at him with loathing and contempt.

Damn it, what if his plan backfired?

What if, in attempting to finish the business side of things and move onto the personal, he finished them completely?

'I'm not threatening you; I'm giving you an opportunity to come out of this deal a winner.'

Her scornful look burned a hole straight through to his conscience. 'You're trying to buy me off to get what you want. And if I don't comply, you go ahead and offer the council twice what the land is worth by the end of today?'

She shook her head, golden curls rioting around her face and a perfect contrast for the faint pink staining her cheeks. 'Some "opportunity".'

'This deal has to go through. Today,' he said, feeling

like a heel when the fire drained from her eyes only to be replaced by fear.

'I need some more time.'

Her whispered plea slammed into his soul, raising questions he'd rather ignore.

Was his dream more important than hers?

Did he care enough about her to turn his back on his own future?

If he cared, how much?

And what was he going to do about it?

'Time isn't going to help.'

Either of them. He needed to get out of Vance Corporation, she needed to start a new gallery elsewhere with the money he was determined she would have. And they needed to recreate the fire that had consumed them both last night, repeatedly.

'You don't know that. There's the National Trust, the Victorian Arts Council…' She trailed off, the truth finally dawning in her stricken eyes. 'You've already made the offer, haven't you?'

Cooper hesitated, knowing he couldn't lie to the woman he loved yet aware the truth would potentially ruin what little chance they had for a future.

The woman he loved?

He slumped in his chair, the words echoing through his head like a gunshot.

He loved her…he loved her…he loved her…

It couldn't be.

No way.

His mind must've slipped up under the strain, substituting the L word for caring.

Yeah, that sounded better. He cared for her.

Much better.

Yet when he met her defeated stare, unshed tears glistening green, his heart made a mockery of his head.

For a guy who thrived on cool, hard facts, who used logic to sort through everything, an emotion he had little time for had snuck up and whacked him a beauty.

The longer Ariel stared at him, the worse his heart clenched till it took every ounce of will-power not to leap from his chair and cradle her in his arms.

'Tell me the truth.'

Cooper started, shocked to think she'd seen right through him in his moment of revelation before realising she meant the truth about his offer to the council. He could've sagged with relief if the thought that what he was about to say would probably rob him of any chance to express his newly discovered feelings ever.

Taking a deep breath, he selected his words carefully. 'I have approached the council and had discussions about the sale of land but nothing has been formalised.'

'But you've basically thrown more money at them than they know what to do with, right? So if I don't accept your offer now and sell out before the lease is up, they're going to jump at it pretty much straight away?'

He nodded, hating the defeated slump to her shoulders, the shaking hand that fiddled with a curl near her right ear, winding it furiously around and around till he thought it would snap off.

'So what was the extra time about? Giving me another twenty-four hours to stew before I finally capitulate to Mr Big-Shot and make his day?'

Scorn dripped from every word and she straightened, anger replacing defeat in her eyes.

That's my girl, he thought, admiring her fighting spirit yet wishing he weren't the one to instigate it.

'I want you to do this of your own accord, to make the decision yourself.'

She laughed, a harsh, hollow sound that had nothing to do with happiness. 'That's rich coming from you.' Tapping her temple, she looked heavenward as if deep in thought. 'Let me see. I get to make my own decision as long as it's by the end of today. Thanks so much.'

'We're going round in circles here. That's my final offer and, as a smart businesswoman, I think you should take it.'

Though it wasn't his final offer, not if he had any say. Once this whole mess got sorted and they could put business behind them, he had a whole host of other offers in mind, the main one being a relationship.

He didn't have a whole lot of experience with love.

He'd loved his mum; she'd died when he was too young.

He loved his dad; he might as well have died.

No, love wasn't a reliable emotion, but one thing was for certain; he loved Ariel and he'd make damn sure he gave it his best shot.

Her steady green-eyed gaze locked on his. 'Why is this deal so important to you? You've used words like imperative. I just don't get why a ruthless businessman like you would fluff around for a couple of weeks, posing almost naked, going out for coffees, attending art shows and the like when you could've shafted me right from the start. What's with that?'

Cooper bit back an ironic smile. Here was his big chance to hint at his burgeoning feelings.

And get the same reaction he'd had last night before they'd had sensational sex? No way. Making a total ass of himself twice in less than twenty-four hours wasn't his style.

He settled for semi-truth. It was the least he could do considering she'd stood up to everything he'd thrown at her and then some.

'This deal is my ticket out of here. It's something I've been planning towards for a while now and I really need to make it happen.'

Her lips twisted in a cynical smile. 'Why? Aren't they paying you enough? Not enough perks? The boss got you over a barrel? Though with a name like Vance Corporation, I'm guessing you like to keep it all in the family.'

All in the family.

Ironic, considering he'd lost the bulk of his family, his dad, that fateful day almost a year ago when he'd signed on the dotted line, blown away to be working with someone of Eric's reputation.

'My father's the CEO,' Cooper said. And all his dad cared about these days was making money, acquiring prime land, developing properties. And all at the expense of the things that used to matter to him, like fishing, four-wheel driving and hanging out with his son.

Despite Cooper's drive to leave Vance Corp behind, he knew he'd miss his dad. Cooper hadn't given up on him completely. Maybe his dad would remember the old saying 'absence makes the heart grow fonder' and make an effort to patch things up once he left?

He hoped so but he wouldn't hold his breath.

Ariel quirked an eyebrow, losing none of her sass despite the anger tightening her exquisite features. 'So it can't be the pay or the perks that's the problem if daddy holds the purse strings. What is it? The executive bathroom not up to scratch? You've lost your car park?'

'It's time for me to go it alone. You of all people should understand that.'

'Oh.'

Ariel blushed and practically squirmed in her seat, and he held up his hand to ward off whatever she was about to say when she opened her mouth.

'My motivation is irrelevant. What needs to be done right now is you placing your signature on the dotted line before five o'clock today. That's all that matters.'

He rustled papers and, along with his brisk tone, hoped that gave her the message. He needed to concentrate on the business at hand, get away from the sensitive topic of his motivation. The momentary concern he'd glimpsed in her eyes had him wanting to blurt out the whole sorry tale just to get it off his chest.

But he couldn't. He was a guy, a tough Aussie bloke, a man's man. He would stifle his feelings and get on with things. His dad's mantra, not his.

And for the last year, he'd thought his dad's mantra sucked.

'All that matters?' she muttered, grabbing her bag and leaping from her chair as if she'd sat on hot coals. 'What matters is that you're a selfish, spoiled rich boy who always gets what he wants. You don't care about who gets trampled on the way or whose dreams your ruin. And to think I was actually feeling for you a few seconds ago, about the whole going-it-alone, doing-it-tough thing!'

'I don't need your pity.'

He shot to his feet, torn between wanting to blurt the truth and sending her packing for her damning character assessment. Though at that moment, he didn't know what rankled more: the fact she thought so poorly of him or the tiny niggle of truth in what she'd said.

He was selfish.

He did want this deal to go through, whatever the cost.

But what if it cost him the woman he loved?

'I guess not. A guy like you wouldn't need anything from a girl like me. Besides sex, of course, and now that you've got that it's back to business as usual.'

He was surprised it had taken her this long to mention what had happened at her place last night. He'd been grateful for it, preferring to keep this a business discussion and totally separate from the other important issue: them.

'That's not fair. We talked about what happened last night before I left this morning. It has nothing to do with this.'

'You would say that.'

Her scathing look of condemnation kicked him in the guts before she twirled on her heel and headed for the door.

'Last night was incredible, Ariel, and you know it. Don't spoil it by bringing business into it.'

She hesitated at the door but she didn't turn around.

Damn it, the sooner this deal went through, the sooner he could move on to more important things such as showing this stubborn, beautiful woman just how much she meant to him.

'This needs to be finalised, Ariel. Today.'

She ignored him and strutted out the door, slamming it in her wake, a hollow, empty sound that reverberated through his soul as he realised she'd probably just slammed the door on any chance of a future between them.

'What's all the ruckus about?'

Eric barged into Cooper's office, shirt sleeves rolled up to the elbows, tie-less and with a killer crease in his navy trousers, his usual work garb. His father never conformed, though he expected nothing less than perfection in his employees.

Cooper sank into his chair and gestured for his dad to take the seat Ariel had just vacated. 'Ariel Wallace was just in here.'

Cooper held up his hand to forestall his dad's usual interrogation. 'The deal will be done by the close of business today.'

'Good.'

Cooper struggled not to gape at his dad's one-word, one-syllable answer without a hint of emotion. He'd expected cartwheels from the man who had been after the last bit of prime land in Fitzroy since for ever.

However, what shocked him more was the uncomfortable, almost sad look on his dad's creased face. It resembled the expression he'd worn after his mum's funeral, the same devastated, lost look that came with realising you would never see that person again, would never talk to that person again or share a hug or a laugh with them again.

'What's up? You don't sound so thrilled.'

Cooper expected his dad to give him the brush-off, the usual 'back to business' gruff response he normally got.

His dad ran a hand through his thick thatch of peppery grey hair, his gaze darting around the room as if he wanted to look anywhere but at him.

'Guess I can't change your mind about leaving?'

'No, Dad. You can't,' Cooper said, deliberately keeping his voice devoid of emotion.

Close on the heels of his draining confrontation with Ariel—and the stunning realisation he loved her—he didn't need this.

He'd waited long enough, hoping his dad would broach the yawning gap between them. He'd given his all to Vance Corporation, playing the dutiful son, trying to prove his worth rather than live off the family name, but it looked as if his best efforts weren't good enough.

Nothing he could do or say would ever be good enough and he'd stuck around way too long already. Time to cut his losses and run. And hope to God that his dad would realise what he'd lost when he wasn't around every day.

'That's the first time you've called me that in a long time,' Eric said, his gaze finally coming to rest on his face, the wavering uncertainty Cooper glimpsed there surprising him.

His father was never uncertain about anything.

Ruthless, domineering and pushy, yes.

Uncertain and wavering? No way.

Probably the old man's last-ditch effort to make him stay on at Vance Corp.

'You haven't exactly encouraged familial bonds since I joined the company,' Cooper said, opting for blunt honesty to get this over and done with. No use re-hashing the last year now.

Once again, his dad surprised him. Rather than blustering his way out of an unwelcome topic and changing the subject quick smart, his dad seemed to crumple before his eyes: slumped shoulders, head slouched forward, mouth slack with pain.

'Look, forget I said anything—'

'No.'

His dad's head snapped up and some of the familiar fire blazed in his dark eyes. 'You're right. I don't blame you for not calling me Dad. I've pushed you away. I've made a mess of everything.'

Cooper didn't respond, considering he agreed with everything his dad had just said. Besides, his dad had a look he hadn't seen in twelve months, a look that he genuinely cared about Cooper enough to want to talk to him about something other than business.

'I thought I'd never recover from losing your mother but having you got me through her death. You were my world. Then you started working here…' Eric drifted off, pain glazing his eyes and accentuating the multitude of lines fanning out from their corners.

'But that's what you wanted,' Cooper said, confusion lending a sharp edge to his words.

'I know.'

His dad raised pain-stricken eyes to his, his mouth twisted into a grimace.

'Then why?'

Cooper didn't have to add, Why ignore me? Why treat me like dirt? Why act like I didn't exist, like I wasn't your son any more?

'Because I'm an old fool. A gutless old fool who saw his life flash before his eyes the minute you sealed your first deal. I'm jealous, son. I've been so jealous I couldn't see straight. Throw in the fear that I'll soon be redundant, and the fact you keep negotiating deals I can't seem to seal these days, and there you have it.'

'You're jealous?' Cooper shook his head, knowing there had to be more to it. 'That's it?'

His dad sagged before his eyes. 'Age does stupid things to a man. I was bursting with pride when you first signed up then within two months I wanted to boot you straight out the door.'

'Then why the contract? Why not let me go months ago when I wanted to?'

Eric looked away. 'Because you're great for the company. You've brought more business in over the last year than I have in the last five years. I pushed you harder, knowing you wouldn't disappoint.'

'You took advantage of the fact your son wouldn't tell you to shove it,' Cooper said, stunned to discover the reason behind his dad's animosity, feeling as if he was still missing a major piece of the puzzle.

'There's something else.'

Cooper leaned forward, not sure if he'd heard Eric's whispered words.

'What?'

'A guilty conscience,' his dad said, shaking his head, sorrow ageing him ten years before his eyes. 'Masterson's approached me just after you started here. They were head-hunting you. Heard about the whizkid from uni, knew you were my son, wanted to throw a few spanners Vance Corp's way but wanted to do it right. They were fishing around, wanting to know if you'd signed a binding contract, that sort of thing. All over a friendly beer, of course. They were going to approach you directly after paying me the courtesy visit, but I lied, put them off.'

A light bulb went off in Cooper's mind. 'So that's why you made me sign a contract like everyone else the month after I started?'

Eric nodded, his mouth downturned. 'I told them you were legally bound to Vance Corporation and that was that.'

'Before I signed the contract?'

'Uh-huh.'

'Was their offer any good?'

'Unbelievable.' Eric hesitated, wringing his hands before continuing. 'I'm sorry, son. I was selfish, wanting you to carry on the family tradition, then when I had you where I wanted you, I couldn't handle your success. Stupid, irrational, call it what you like. I'm an idiot.'

Cooper digested the information, knowing he should feel more angry, more deceived. Instead, a strange feeling of relief seeped through him. He finally knew the truth and it had nothing to do with him.

'I know I've treated you like crap, but I want you to know that I'm damn proud of you, Coop.'

Finally, his dad met his gaze and, thankfully, the spark had returned. If anything, the dark eyes glowed with fervour as if daring him to disagree, to challenge. Instead, Cooper smiled.

'You know, for a smart guy, you've made some pretty dumb judgement calls, but I'm willing to forgive and forget if you'll do one thing.'

'What's that?' His dad glared at him with some of his characteristic suspicion and Cooper's smile widened.

'Go fishing with me this weekend. Have a beer or two, just like old times.'

'You're on, son.'

Eric's grin matched his and Cooper shook his head, wishing they'd had this conversation months ago.

'Does this mean you're staying?'

'Don't push your luck, old man.'

Though his dad had posed a valid question.

Today was the first time he'd really looked at his dad in a long time and he didn't like the changes. His dad looked older, more fragile than he had in ages and maybe now wasn't a great time to spread his wings and leave the Vance nest, particularly as it looked as if re-establishing bonds would be high on both their priority lists for a while.

Eric held up both hands as if warding him off. 'Fine, fine, no harm in trying. By the way, is there something going on between you and the Wallace woman?'

Cooper hesitated a second before answering. 'No, why do you ask?'

It wasn't a completely untruthful answer, considering Ariel would probably never speak to him again after today.

His dad shrugged. 'Just a hunch, by the doomsday look on your face when I first came in here and by the tears streaming down her face as she raced out of here after slamming your door.'

'A difference of opinion,' Cooper said, his heart stuttering at the thought of Ariel crying over what he'd done.

'Looked more like a lovers' tiff than a difference of opinion over a business deal to me.'

His dad paused, giving him ample opportunity to deny it. Cooper merely clamped his lips together.

'Then again, what do I know? I'm a stupid old fool and now we both know it.'

His dad rose to his feet, pushed his shirt sleeves

higher and stuck out his hand, looking like the confident Eric of old. 'You know I'm proud of you, Son.'

'Thanks, Dad.'

Cooper shook hands with his dad and shared a smile, a smile filled with hope for their future, before his dad sent him a half-salute and strode out of the office, leaving Cooper to decide how big a mistake he'd made with Ariel and how he could rectify it.

CHAPTER THIRTEEN

ARIEL dabbed her paintbrush in the crimson daub on her palette and made great slashing movements across the canvas propped on the easel in front of her.

Red, the colour of anger and fury.

She followed up with a dab and slash of ebony.

Black, the colour of darkness and gloom.

Another slash, this time with sunshine yellow.

Yellow, the colour of that lily-livered, no-good Cooper Vance's belly, the coward.

She slashed away, combining the colours in a frightening free-for-all in a painting that would never see the light of day but was soothing to her battered soul nonetheless.

The colours summed up her mood perfectly. She'd never felt as angry, gloomy or scared as she did right now, the afternoon she would lose her dream. Not to mention renege on a promise that she'd vowed to keep till her dying day.

Cooper Vance was evil.

Pure, unadulterated evil.

He'd used her, schmoozing up to her, acting like a friend, playing on her emotions, initiating her into the best sex she'd ever had in her life, making her love him and all for what? To whip the gallery right out from under her nose anyway.

What Cooper wanted, Cooper got and she'd been justified in calling him a selfish, spoiled brat earlier. She just wished she'd had the guts to say more.

Slumping forward, she rested her forehead against the canvas, not caring about the instant oil-paint tattoo imprinted there.

She'd never felt so alone, so defeated…and in the midst of her absolute misery a thought so profound, so awful, pierced her gloom.

What had she thought a few seconds ago? Something about *making her love him*?

She loved him? Was she out of her mind?

Uh-uh.

No way.

No how.

Must be the stress sending her insane. She'd heard about people going crazy with post-traumatic stress disorder. Maybe her bout had set in early?

She couldn't love him.

He was obnoxious, self-centred and a know-it-all Mr Big-Shot.

He had insinuated his way into her life and got under her skin before flaying it off her with cold, calculated precision, all in the name of sealing his precious deal.

The very idea she could love a guy like that was preposterous.

But what if you do?

'Oh, heck,' she muttered, sitting bolt upright and

staring blankly at the vivid canvas, wishing she could turn the clock back a few minutes and wipe out her thoughts.

For, once the question had been raised by her stupid inner self, she knew without a doubt what the answer was and it made her want to head-bang the canvas repeatedly in the hope it would knock some sense into her.

'*Bella*, you here?'

Ariel hadn't heard the chimes signalling Sofia's entrance to the gallery—probably all those insane inner voices whispering silly nothings in her head about loving Cooper Vance—and knew she wasn't in the mood for a chat.

Maybe if she pleaded a headache she could get rid of her friend, close up for the day and harass some poor courier to deliver a bomb along with the signed papers to Cooper?

The stupid proposal she had no option now but to sign thanks to the traitorous louse's deadline.

'Out the back, Sofia,' she called out, cleaning her brushes and palette out of habit rather than a driving necessity to do so.

Besides, she needed something to do with her hands other than put the finishing flourish on the document signalling her ultimate demise.

'Bella! How are you?'

Sofia bustled into the studio, dressed in head-to-toe fuchsia and sporting a hat that could take out a person's eye at twenty paces.

Ariel turned from the sink and rubbed her hands down the front of her smock. 'Actually, I have a headache.'

To her surprise, Sofia laughed rather than cooed in

concern. 'Must be all that paint seeping into your brain,' she said, pointing to her forehead and beaming, her perfectly capped teeth in stark contrast to the bright pink of her dress.

Ariel managed a rueful smile as she picked up a nearby rag and swiped at her forehead. 'I forgot in all the excitement.'

'Excitement?'

Sofia's nose twitched at the faintest hint of gossip and right now, her nostrils fairly quivered.

'Yes, the excitement of trying out a new technique. I read about this tribe in Africa who only paint with their heads so thought I'd try it out. Want to see the results?'

Ariel's smile broadened at the confused expression on Sofia's exquisitely made-up face. In a way, Sofia's impromptu visit had achieved a miracle already. She'd smiled when a few minutes earlier it had felt as if she'd never smile again.

'*Mamma mia*!'

Sofia's hands flew to her mouth as she stared at the canvas, her shocked gaze darting between the painting and Ariel's face and back again.

'You don't like?'

'It's horrible, *bella*! Nasty. Angry. Ugly. No, no, no, this is not you at all.'

Ariel stood alongside Sofia and stared at the canvas, the vivid streaks of red, black and yellow telling an emotional story she couldn't hide.

'I take it you don't want to buy this one for your collection?'

Ariel stepped away from the painting, finding it suddenly depressing. Usually, painting was a way to express herself, a way to feel good about the world, a cathartic experience, but somehow seeing the angry slashes of vibrant paint saddened her and reminded her exactly why she'd picked up the brush on the return from Cooper's office.

She'd needed to debrief, to offload, to express one iota of the devastation wreaking havoc on her psyche, and painting had been her only option.

Sadly, it hadn't helped and now she had to allay Sofia's qualms before she blabbed the whole sorry tale to her friend.

'What is it, *bella*? What is the problem?' Sofia grabbed both her hands and squeezed, her coal-black eyes beseeching, a frown creasing her brow.

'No problem,' Ariel said, using every ounce of self-control not to fall into Sofia's arms a babbling mess.

'Is it money? You need more than what the commission brought you? I can give it to you right now!' Sofia dropped her hands long enough to scramble in her handbag for the cheque book Ariel knew she always kept on her 'in case of a bargain'.

Ariel laid a hand on Sofia's arm, stilling the scrambling woman. 'I don't need money—' *I need a miracle* '—but thanks for offering.'

'You sure?' Sofia didn't seem reassured, her penetrating stare sweeping Ariel's face with the vigour of a bloodhound getting a sniff of a trail.

'I'm sure.'

Ariel could never ask Sofia for the money to buy out the lease on the gallery. She would never risk their precious friendship over a loan she had no way of repaying. Aunt Barb had taught her many things, one of them being never borrow more than you can repay, and she'd adhered to that policy her entire life, which explained why she didn't own a car, had no mortgage and paid her rent on time.

Until now.

'Okay. In that case, I dropped by to invite you over for dinner tomorrow night.'

Sofia paused, a sly grin spreading across her face. 'And I thought you might like to bring that delightful young man of yours? He likes lasagna, no?'

'No!'

Ariel knew her reaction was over the top but the mere thought of Cooper made her want to retch.

'No?'

Ariel calmed her voice with effort. 'What I mean is, Cooper isn't my young man. He's busy with work and I'm busy here so we won't be seeing much of each other any more.'

Try never. Which would be too soon for her.

Sofia's mouth drooped. 'Oh, no, what a shame. Such a nice boy. Such manners, such class, so handsome.'

Nice boy? Ariel tried not to choke on the lump of disgust suddenly lodged in her throat.

'Ah-h-h…now I understand.' Sofia pointed at the painting and grimaced. 'You are very sad about not seeing him any more. You love him and you are pining for him. It all makes sense now.'

'I don't love him!'

But the moment the denial left her lips, Ariel knew it wasn't just the thought of losing the gallery that made her want to weep into the next century but the thought of losing Cooper too that added to her pain.

For once, Sofia didn't push or probe or offer a ten-minute matchmaking lecture.

'Don't worry, *bella*. It will all work out in the end.'

However, as Sofia wrapped her in a smothering hug Ariel seriously doubted it.

Cooper paced outside the entrance to the National Gallery, oblivious to the stunning fountains, the impressive lead light windows and the natural beauty of the Royal Botanic Gardens opposite.

He had a lot on his mind, namely a stubborn, gorgeous artist and whether she'd give him a chance to explain.

It had all seemed so clear after he'd sorted things out with his dad and he hadn't wasted a second in putting his plan into action. He just hoped the wheels in motion wouldn't be derailed by the fiery blonde harridan who had captured his heart without trying.

At that moment, he saw Ariel alight from a tram on St Kilda Road and he exhaled in relief.

She came.

Then again, she would have considering she thought she was meeting a representative of the Victorian Arts Council rather than the selfish brat she'd accused him of being earlier today.

His pulse raced and his heart turned over as she waited at the traffic lights, a stunning figure in crazy striped knickerbockers, a flowing purple top and towering cork wedges that tied around her ankles with black satin ribbon. The mix would've looked silly on any other woman. On her, it looked amazing.

She had an inner grace, a special glow that made anything on her or around her take on special significance, and he'd been mad enough to almost let her slip through his fingers.

Thank God he'd come to his senses. Now, if only she'd give him a chance to prove exactly how much she meant to him.

Cooper waited in the lengthening shadows as early dusk fell over Melbourne, watching Ariel's every step with increasing impatience.

This had to work.

It had to.

Ariel glanced at her watch as she reached the entrance to the gallery, relieved to see she'd made it with a minute to spare.

This could be it, her one and only opportunity to save Colour by Dreams. And a golden opportunity to rip up the document burning a hole in her carryall; the signed document that she hadn't couriered to Cooper once the Arts Council's director's summons had arrived.

She hadn't questioned the timely request. Instead, she preferred to see it as a sign that her luck was changing for the better. Besides, the director had been at Chelsea's showing and maybe he wanted to discuss the future of Victorian art and the part she—and her gallery—could play in it.

She closed her eyes and made a fervent wish that she was right in her assumptions.

However, the minute she opened them again and found herself staring into Cooper's too-blue eyes she knew that wishes didn't come true. At least not to her.

'What are you doing here?' she spat out, gripping her bag tightly to prevent herself from swinging it at him, her first crazy impulse when she saw his handsome face.

'There's something you should see inside,' he said, his well-modulated voice raising her hackles.

Why couldn't he be more ruffled, more scruffy, less polite, less perfect?

She felt gauche and unworldly and flawed next to him and she hated it. If his mere presence here hadn't undermined her, his air of cool unflappability would have. Drat the man.

She stuck a hand on one hip and tossed him an 'I don't give a damn' look.

'And what would that be? A picture of you in all your smug glory because you've won?'

She paused and tapped her lip with a chewed fingernail, as if deep in thought. 'Though that can't be right. As high as the gallery ceilings are, I doubt they could fit a portrait of your big head in there.'

To her chagrin, he didn't react apart from a slight twitch at the corners of his mouth.

That very kissable mouth, the same mouth that had worked its magic on her and coerced her into believing a whole lot of garbage, mainly that she loved him.

She had to be nuts.

'Look, this will only take a few minutes. What have you got to lose?'

'Everything,' she muttered, casting longing glances at the departing tram she'd just disembarked from and shuffling uncertainly from foot to foot before shrugging and making a beeline for the gallery, not caring if Cooper fell into step beside her or not.

She waited till they'd entered the cool interior and moved away from the door before confronting him.

'The director's not coming, is he? This was yet another of your sick power plays to get me to jump to your tune.'

It was a statement, not a question, and she wondered why she'd followed him in here knowing that fact.

Because you love him.

Because you still harbour some crazy hope this is all a bad dream and you'll wake up to a perfect day.

Because you're creative and are way too good at building ridiculous fantasies of happily ever after in your own head!

The great dolt had the grace to look sheepish. 'No, the director isn't coming. I'm sorry about that. It was the only thing I could think of on the spur of the moment to get you here.'

'What for? To rub my nose in it? To make sure I'd meet your stupid deadline?'

The silly thing was, he *was* rubbing her nose in it; rubbing her nose in the fact she loved him. Loved the way his blue eyes shone with intelligence, loved the way his mouth quirked when he was struggling not to laugh, loved the way he filled out a suit, even if guys in fancy rags didn't usually do it for her.

Ariel grabbed for a curl and twisted it around her finger, hoping the sharp tug on her scalp might erase her thoughts. Instead, it made her focus on Cooper even more, the way he reached out to still her hand before thinking better of it and letting his arm drop to his side.

The truth of the matter was that she loved him, loved everything about him, and getting over him would be yet another burden while she tried to recover from the loss of the gallery.

'I asked you here to give you this.'

He reached into the inside pocket of his silk-lined jacket and pulled out a folded document.

'Don't tell me. You've made another amendment and demanded my soul as well.'

He didn't flinch, he didn't speak, but something about the hurt expression in his eyes made her feel lower than an ant's belly.

'Why don't you take a look?'

Rolling her eyes like an adolescent taking a lousy report from a teacher, she snatched the offending document and opened it, prepared to skim the print before folding it and flinging it back in Mr Big-Shot's face.

However, her nasty intentions went up in smoke the minute her eyes focussed on the new owner of the gallery.

'What the—'

She blinked, made a frantic grab at the recently released curl and wound it furiously around her finger over and over, seeing the print but not quite believing it.

'It's yours,' he said, shrugging his broad shoulders as if he purchased galleries for exorbitant amounts of money and bestowed them on needy artists every day.

She shook her head, read the final few lines of the document again, before lifting her head and staring at him in open-mouthed shock. 'This is some kind of joke, right?'

'Of course not. I know how much the gallery means to you. This way, you won't have to worry about losing it ever again.'

He spoke so calmly, so rationally, as if the *fait accompli* of presenting her with sale papers for the gallery bearing her name as owner were nothing out of the ordinary.

'I don't get it.'

Ariel took a deep breath and exhaled slowly, hoping the oxygen rush would clear her head.

It didn't.

She propped against a nearby wall, needing some support at her back before she crumpled in an undignified heap.

If the realisation that she loved Cooper had put her in a spin, it was nothing on the mind-numbing revelation that he'd bought the gallery for her. The big question was why?

'Look, I worked a few things out this afternoon and I thought you'd appreciate the gesture. As much as you want to deny it, I think we have a chance at being more than friends in the future and I wanted you to give us a go without worrying about business stuff.'

More than friends…more than friends…

Suddenly, the befuddled fog clouding Ariel's mind lifted and with a flash of blinding clarity she knew exactly why Mr Big-Shot had got so generous. And the resulting knowledge made her want to retch.

'I'm not for sale,' she said, each word uttered with icy precision as she handed him back the document that burned her fingertips with its treachery. 'So we had sex? Big deal. It doesn't mean you can buy me for a few more cheap thrills. Nice to know what you think of me, though.'

Anger flared in the deep blue depths of Cooper's eyes, sending sapphire shards of fury outwards. 'Don't be ridiculous. I'm not trying to buy you. I just want this damn business sorted out so we can get on with things.'

'What things?' She kept her tone silky smooth when, in fact, she longed to knee him where it hurt the most.

He grabbed hold of her upper arms before she could react, his offer fluttering to the floor between them. 'Don't pretend there's been nothing between us. You feel the sparks just as much as I do. Is it so wrong to want to explore that further? To see whether there's a chance for a couple like us?'

Ariel tried to wriggle out of his vice-like grip but couldn't move, trapped in the intensity of his stare, wishing he still didn't have the power to make her pulse race and her heart turn over.

'There's no chance.'

And the knowledge stabbed her anew. They were too different, too conflicted and his actions today spoke for themselves. When the going got tough, he bought his way out of a situation.

For guys like Cooper Vance, money talked.

Unfortunately, she wouldn't listen. She couldn't.

She'd learned long ago, that no matter how desperate or hungry or cold, there was always a line you shouldn't cross. And right now, Cooper had unwittingly drawn that line and she wouldn't cross it.

If nothing else, she still had her pride.

Shrugging out of his grasp, she rummaged through her carryall till she found what she was looking for.

'Here. I think this is what you want.'

She slapped the signed proposal in his hand and closed his fingers over it.

Cooper shook his head and tried to give it back to her. 'This isn't what I want. What I want is you.'

Pain, fierce and deep, twisted her gut till she almost

cried out with the agony of it. 'Like I already said, I'm not for sale.'

Without waiting a second longer, Ariel turned on her heel and walked quickly towards the exit, praying her tears wouldn't turn to sobs before she made it out the front door.

'Ariel, wait!'

Ignoring Cooper's desperate plea, she picked up the pace, wishing she'd worn her ballet flats rather than three-inch wedges today. That was all she needed, to break an ankle to match her broken heart.

'Please, Ariel. I need you.'

Her steps slowed as she reached the far end of the plush foyer. The front door was in sight and she could've made a bolt for it. Instead, the minute Cooper laid a hand on her shoulder, she swivelled to face him, unsure whether to swing it at him or rummage in her bag for a wad of tissues.

'What did you just say?'

She tilted her head up, ignoring the tears pouring down her face as she eyeballed the jerk responsible for them.

'I need you.'

He reached up and, with infinite tenderness, wiped the tears from her cheeks with his thumbs.

'I need you. I want you. I can't imagine my life without you.'

Once his thumbs stilled, he cupped her face, staring into her eyes as if he meant every word.

As if.

Looked as if he would pull out every weapon in his arsenal to win this contest.

If he couldn't buy her, he'd schmooze her, just as he had right from the very beginning.

'There's a word for what you're experiencing. Insanity.'

'You think I'm crazy? Fine.'

He dropped his hands to clasp hers, holding on so tight her fingers went numb. 'Tell me what you see.'

His soft, husky tone took her back to the exact moment she'd asked him the same thing, his disappointing answer and the realisation at the time of the yawning gap between them.

The sad thing was, nothing had changed since that day in the gallery when she'd done her best to show him what sort of a person she was, what was important to her.

Cooper only saw what he wanted to see and that would never change. For him, the world was black and white, a place filled with money and property and fancy cars, a world she could never belong or feel comfortable in no matter how serious his intentions.

'Let me go—'

'Tell me what you see.'

He squeezed her hands, his steady gaze not leaving hers for a second.

She rolled her eyes, knowing she had to put an end to this fiasco sooner rather than later. Her heart had already fragmented a few minutes ago when he'd thought he could buy her, no use letting it shatter altogether and do permanent damage to her insides.

'Fine. You want to know what I see? I see a big-headed, overconfident, pompous jerk who thinks he can buy everything he wants.'

He didn't blink.

He didn't flinch.

And Ariel found herself battling tears again at the

cruel words she'd just uttered all in the name of severing all ties with the guy she loved once and for all.

'Want to know what I see?'

'Not really.'

Her defiant act would've worked better if her breath hadn't hitched and come out sounding like a pathetic sob.

'I'll tell you anyway.'

To her amazement, he smiled, a soft, gentle smile totally at odds with his usual arrogance and it almost undid her completely.

'I see a beautiful woman filled with fire and passion and conviction. A woman who gives her all to keep a promise. A woman who steals my breath away with how much I love her...'

He trailed off and for a moment Ariel wondered if her frazzled brain had conjured up the words she'd wanted to hear.

He tugged on their linked hands and she leaned towards him, powerless to stop the swift, fierce kiss he slanted across her lips as if branding her as his.

'You love me?' she murmured, pulling back to stare at his face while wishing he'd kiss her again and again till she didn't have to think any more.

He nodded, his blue eyes glowing with an emotion that could only be love, its warmth radiating towards her better than any roaring log fire and infusing her with a bone-melting heat.

'I love you. All of you, from that over-stressed curl you keep winding around your finger to the bottoms of those crazy shoes you wear and every delicious inch in between. I love you, Ariel Wallace. So what do you think about that?'

He placed a finger under her chin and tipped it up, his gaze drifting to her lips.

'I think you've been spending too much time at the studio and those paint fumes have affected you as much as they've affected me.'

The corners of his delightful mouth twitched. 'Does that mean—'

'Yes. It does. I love you too. Don't ask me why because we're as opposite as two people can get but, somehow, I've fallen for you.'

'Such sincere words of love,' he teased, placing her hand on his heart with his hand covering it.

Ariel smiled right back, enjoying the fact his heart pumped as hard and fast as hers and wondering exactly how much faster their organs could take when they moved past the kissing part onto the good stuff again. The thought alone sent her into meltdown.

'You know I'll still paint and run the gallery and wear funky fashion?'

He dropped a slow, lingering kiss on her lips, the type of kiss that had her melding to him and wishing their clothes would disappear and they could find themselves miraculously in a private place.

'You know I'll still acquire land and develop properties and wear suits and ties?'

She shrugged, staring up at him from beneath her lashes. 'I suppose I can learn to live with it.'

'Ah-h-h…but can you learn to live with this?'

His hot, open-mouthed kiss had her hankering for more, a lifetime more.

EPILOGUE

'I NOW declare the Barbara Kane Art School officially open.'

Sofia cut the thick red ribbon stretched across the front of the new building with great aplomb before spoiling her regal act by grabbing a glass of champagne from Chelsea and guzzling it.

Ariel laughed and leaned back, content in the circle of Cooper's arms as they watched Sofia and Chelsea take charge of the milling crowd and guide them through the glass doors of the new school.

'You made this happen, you know,' she said, snuggling into her husband's arms further as a cold gust of wind blew up Brunswick Street.

'We both did,' Cooper murmured against her ear, hugging her tight as his hands skimmed the sensitive underside of her breasts and made her shiver more than any old southerly wind.

She turned in the circle of his arms and looked up, amazed that the man staring down with so much love was her husband.

'Barb would've been so proud.'

He stroked her cheek with slow gentleness. 'She would've been proud of you.'

Ariel blinked back the sudden tears, remembering a morning years earlier when a compassionate woman had taken pity on a down-and-out street kid.

'She took a chance on me when no one else would. Barb saw something in me I never knew existed. I owe her so much.'

A flicker of remorse shot through Cooper's eyes. 'I had no idea about your past and how much the gallery meant to you or how hard I must've seemed, pushing you relentlessly, forcing you to sell—'

'Shh...' She placed a finger on his lips, a shiver of delight skittling down her spine when he nibbled it. 'Old news. Look how far we've come.'

He glanced around them, noticed the absent crowd and pulled her further into the shade of an old oak. 'Tell me, Mrs Vance. Exactly how far have we come?'

He kissed his way from her finger to her wrist and slid his lips up her arm till her head fell back in abandon, yearning for his masterful touch on the sensitive spot between neck and collar-bone.

'Oh...' she murmured, melting into his arms, knowing she'd never felt so safe, so treasured, as she did in his embrace.

A tooting horn disrupted their erotic encounter and Ariel chuckled at the mortified expression on Cooper's face as he straightened. 'What? Doesn't Mr Big-Shot get caught out necking with his wife?'

'I have a reputation in the business world to uphold,' he said, aiming for a haughty look, which fell flat considering the smug smile on his face.

'Yeah, you're a real toughie,' she said, gesturing towards the art school over her shoulder with her thumb. 'Not only do you throw yourself wholeheartedly behind the new and improved Colour by Dreams, you find this delightful row of old terrace houses, pay the owners ten times what they're worth and develop them into an art school for underprivileged kids in the area.'

Cooper smiled, a warm, tender smile that never failed to set her pulse racing.

'Hey, it wasn't all me. My dad's a toughie too. After all, it was his idea to get Vance Corporation's employees volunteering down here once a week as part of their better-employee-relations policy.'

Ariel noted the pride in Cooper's voice when he mentioned Eric and she couldn't be happier. She'd watched the two of them re-establish a strong father-son bond over the last few months and had been touched when Eric had included her in a boys' weekend away where the three of them had sat around and she'd learned more about her amazing husband from a man proud to tell a lifetime of anecdotes.

'What are you thinking?'

Cooper slid his hands around her waist and locked them behind her back, bringing their lower halves into tantalising contact and making her wonder how soon till they could escape to the cosy confines of her studio, one of their favourite places for making love.

It had all started there and, thankfully, Cooper had agreed to pose for her again, completely naked this time, though she never quite got around to painting him.

He had a way of distracting her that made every colour

she'd ever imagined coalesce into brilliant, startling clarity as he took her to the stars and back every time.

Smiling at her adorable husband, she said, 'I'm thinking you and I are one heck of a team, Mr Big-Shot.'

'I love it when you call me names,' he growled, and proceeded to show her exactly how much.

The big miniseries from

HARLEQUIN *Presents*

Dare you read it?

Bedded by *Blackmail*

Forced to bed...then to wed?

He's got her firmly in his sights and she's got
only one chance of survival—surrender to his
blackmail...and him...in his bed!

THE ITALIAN
RAGS-TO-RICHES WIFE

by *Julia James*
Book # 2716

Laura Stowe has something Allesandro di Vincenzo wants,
and he must grit his teeth and charm her into his bed, where
she will learn the meaning of desire....

Available April 2008 wherever books are sold.

Don't miss more titles in the
BEDDED BY BLACKMAIL series—coming soon!

HARLEQUIN *Presents*

THE DESERT KINGS

**Blood brothers, hot-blooded lovers—
who will they take as their queens?**

These sheikhs are blood brothers, rulers of
all they survey. But though used to impossible
wealth and luxury, they also thrive on the
barbaric beauty of their kingdom. Are there
women with spirit enough to tame these hard,
proud kings and become their lifelong queens?

THE SHEIKH'S CHOSEN QUEEN
by Jane Porter

Jesslyn has been summoned to the desert land
Sheikh Sharif rules. Jesslyn refuses to take orders, but
Sharif is determined: she will obey his command and
submit—to becoming his wife and queen!

Available April 2008 wherever books are sold.

Look on Jane's Web site for more information
on this sizzling miniseries!

Inside ROMANCE

Stay up-to-date on all your
romance reading news!

Inside Romance is a FREE quarterly newsletter
highlighting our upcoming series releases
and promotions.

Visit
www.eHarlequin.com/InsideRomance
to sign up to receive our complimentary newsletter today!

IRN1107

REQUEST YOUR FREE BOOKS!

2 FREE NOVELS PLUS 2 FREE GIFTS!

PASSION GUARANTEED SEDUCTION

YES! Please send me 2 FREE Harlequin Presents® novels and my 2 FREE gifts (gifts are worth about $10). After receiving them, if I don't wish to receive any more books, I can return the shipping statement marked "cancel". If I don't cancel, I will receive 6 brand-new novels every month and be billed just $4.05 per book in the U.S. or $4.74 per book in Canada, plus 25¢ shipping and handling per book and applicable taxes, if any*. That's a savings of close to 15% off the cover price! I understand that accepting the 2 free books and gifts places me under no obligation to buy anything. I can always return a shipment and cancel at any time. Even if I never buy another book, the two free books and gifts are mine to keep forever.

106 HDN ERRW 306 HDN ERRL

Name _____ (PLEASE PRINT)

Address _____ Apt. #

City _____ State/Prov. _____ Zip/Postal Code

Signature (if under 18, a parent or guardian must sign)

Mail to the Harlequin Reader Service:
IN U.S.A.: P.O. Box 1867, Buffalo, NY 14240-1867
IN CANADA: P.O. Box 609, Fort Erie, Ontario L2A 5X3

Not valid to current subscribers of Harlequin Presents books.

Want to try two free books from another line?
Call 1-800-873-8635 or visit www.morefreebooks.com.

* Terms and prices subject to change without notice. N.Y. residents add applicable sales tax. Canadian residents will be charged applicable provincial taxes and GST. This offer is limited to one order per household. All orders subject to approval. Credit or debit balances in a customer's account(s) may be offset by any other outstanding balance owed by or to the customer. Please allow 4 to 6 weeks for delivery. Offer available while quantities last.

Your Privacy: Harlequin Books is committed to protecting your privacy. Our Privacy Policy is available online at www.eHarlequin.com or upon request from the Reader Service. From time to time we make our lists of customers available to reputable third parties who may have a product or service of interest to you. If you would prefer we not share your name and address, please check here. ☐

HP08

HARLEQUIN *Presents*

He's successful, powerful—and extremely sexy....
He also happens to be her boss! Used to getting his
own way, he'll demand what he wants from her—
in the boardroom and the bedroom....

Watch the sparks fly as these couples
work together—and play together!

IN BED WITH
THE BOSS

Don't miss any of the stories in April's collection!

MISTRESS IN PRIVATE
by JULIE COHEN

IN BED WITH HER ITALIAN BOSS
by KATE HARDY

MY TALL DARK GREEK BOSS
by ANNA CLEARY

HOUSEKEEPER TO
THE MILLIONAIRE
by LUCY MONROE

Available April 8
wherever books are sold.